# THE MERCILESS

# THE MERCILESS

## DANIELLE VEGA

razOr
bill

AN IMPRINT OF PENGUIN GROUP (USA)

Penguin.com

Razorbill, an Imprint of Penguin Random House

Produced by Alloy Entertainment
1700 Broadway
New York, NY 10019

Copyright © 2014 Alloy Entertainment

ISBN: 978-1-59514-723-3

Printed in the United States of America

1 3 5 7 9 10 8 6 4 2

Design by Liz Dresner

# THE MERCILESS

# CHAPTER ONE

I snag my thumb on the lunch tray's metal edge, and a crescent of blood appears beneath my cuticle. It oozes into the cracks surrounding my nail, then spills over to one side, forming a perfect red droplet, almost like a tear.

I swear under my breath. The cut stings, but at least I didn't smear blood across my T-shirt. Nothing says "be my friend" like serial-killer stains on the first day of school. A stack of napkins sits next to the bin of plastic silverware, but the guy in the food line in front of me is blocking it.

"Excuse me," I say, and the guy turns around. He's good-looking in that athletic, future-frat-boy way where he doesn't really have to try. His brown hair sticks up all over, and he wears a loose, wrinkled shirt, as if he's just rolled out of bed.

Years of being the new girl have helped me perfect my shy half smile. It's as close as I ever come to flirting. I motion to my bleeding finger. "Can you hand me a napkin?"

"Ouch," the guy says, grabbing a few napkins from the stack. His smile beats mine by a few watts, and I blush.

"Hey, do you need a Band-Aid?" asks a girl behind me, and I turn. She has platinum-blond hair cut short, like a boy's. Oversize black glasses without any lenses sit on her nose, and she wears a neon-pink tank top stretched so thin I can see her black bra through the material. A man's golden ring dangles from a chain around her neck.

"Yeah, thanks," I say. Next to her, my standard first-day uniform of a gray T-shirt and dark jeans looks comically plain. A few schools ago, I tried layering rubber bracelets around my wrists and coloring on my Converse sneakers with Sharpies, but today my wrists are bare, my sneakers brand-new. It's time for a change.

"Hey, Brooklyn, what's up?" The boy nods at her. They don't seem like the kind of people who'd be friends, but his tone is nice enough. Brooklyn slides her tattered backpack off one shoulder and reaches into the front pocket.

"Hiya, Charlie," she says to him. "Your brother miss me yet?"

The name *Charlie* fits the cute, athletic guy, and it makes me like him more than if his name were Zack or Chad. A Charlie helps you find your algebra class when you can't figure out your new class schedule. Chad burps the alphabet.

Charlie runs a hand through his hair, leaving it even messier than before. "*Miss* isn't the word I'd use. . . ."

"Ex-boyfriend?" I interrupt to keep from being left out of the conversation. Asking a million questions is New Girl 101. People love talking about themselves. Brooklyn pulls her hand out of her bag and hands me a clear bandage decorated with a tiny picture of a mustache.

"Ex-boss," she says. "But he'll be begging for me to come back any day now. Hey, cool tat."

She points to the crook of my hand, where I sketched a serpent wearing a headdress made of feathers. It's called Quetzalcoatl. When I was little and my mom and I still visited the tiny town where she grew up in Mexico, my grandmother told stories about Quetzalcoatl. Grandmother's too sick to tell the stories anymore, but I sketch the serpent in my journal sometimes. And on my hand, apparently.

"It's not a real tattoo," I admit, rubbing at the drawing with the palm of my other hand. I'll have to wash it off before my mom sees it. She's never liked Grandmother's religious stories. My mom got her US citizenship five years ago, and she says Grandmother's spooky Mexican folktales remind her of all the reasons she'd wanted to move away. "Just Sharpie."

"Oh." Brooklyn sounds disappointed, but Charlie raises an eyebrow and nods in approval.

"You drew that? Nice," he says.

Before I can respond, a dark-haired girl stops in the middle of the cafeteria and clears her throat. The talking, laughing students around us fall silent, as if they've been placed under a spell.

"Can I have your attention, everyone?" she asks, even though everyone's already looking at her. A group of six or seven people crowd behind her, all holding bags and cardboard boxes.

"Jesus." Brooklyn grimaces, pushing her fake glasses up her nose. Her tone is completely different than it was a second ago, when she offered me the Band-Aid. "Is it time for this shit again?"

"I'm Riley, as most of you know," the dark-haired girl continues in a clear, peppy voice. "And it's time for the annual school food drive for the St. Michael's Soup Kitchen. I hope this year you'll all help me do God's work and bring in food for the homeless. Last year alone, we collected over five hundred cans!"

Students around us start to clap. It takes me by surprise, and I join a beat too late. The only time kids at my last school clapped for people was when they tripped and dropped their lunch trays.

Behind me, Brooklyn makes a gagging sound.

"Come on," Charlie mutters. He'd been clapping with the others, but he breaks off to nudge Brooklyn with his elbow. I bite back a smile. I was wrong; he doesn't really seem like a frat boy after all.

Brooklyn makes a gun with her hand and points it at Riley's head, narrowing her eyes.

"*Pew*," she whispers, shooting an imaginary bullet. She blows smoke from the tips of her fingers.

I raise an eyebrow as I reach past her for a carton of milk. I've hung out with girls like her before, the girls who skip third period to smoke cloves in the bathroom and pierce their ears with safety pins. It's always exciting for a while, but they never become real friends. I usually spend most of my time trying to prove I'm cool enough to hang with them.

Still, beggars can't be choosers. So when Brooklyn winks at me and says "Later," I smile and wave back.

Charlie shakes his head as Brooklyn walks away, and a few strands of floppy brown hair fall over his eyes.

His arm brushes against mine as he leans over the food counter to grab a fork and napkin.

"Don't take Brooklyn seriously," he says, flashing me a half smile. A dimple appears in his cheek. "It's not so bad here, I promise. See you around?"

My heart does a little flip inside my chest as he walks away. I've been bouncing around long enough to know my crushes never turn out the way I want them to, but I still manage to fall in love every time I meet a new guy with a great smile. I should have learned by now that high school romance isn't in the cards for me. My mom's been a medical technician for the army since moving to the States. I'm at a new school every six months, like clockwork.

This time it's Adams High School, in the tiny army town of Friend, Mississippi. Friend feels like the inside of an oven. The grass is brown, I hear insects buzzing wherever I go, and there are more churches in my neighborhood than grocery stores. I've lived in nicer places, but in the end it always comes down to the people. I hesitate near the cafeteria doors and glance back over my shoulder at Charlie. Heat creeps up my neck. This place has potential.

The students at Adams eat lunch outside, so I take my tray through the side door and head toward the bleachers. Adams High is a one-story-high building made of cream-colored brick with mud-brown siding. The classrooms are all outdated, with peeling linoleum floors and rickety desks. In fact, the only impressive part of the whole school is its football field, a deep-green stretch of Astroturf surrounded by shiny silver bleachers. Above the bleachers hangs a blue-and-white sign that reads ADAMS HIGH SPARTANS. A Mississippi flag billows in the air next to it.

As I look around for a place to sit, a gasp of hot wind blows my curls into my face. I lift a hand to push them away, immediately noticing the smell. It's like milk gone bad, or moldy cheese.

I take a step toward the bleachers, and the smell gets worse. Now it's chicken that's been in the garbage all night, fish left out in the heat. I pull my T-shirt over my nose and make my way under the bleachers.

That's when I see it.

It's a cat. A dead cat. Skin's been peeled away from the cat's body in strips. Flies buzz around its head and inside its mouth, crawling over its tongue and teeth. Red paint clings to the stiff grass beneath the cat's body, and candles surround it, cemented to the ground in pools of black wax. It takes a minute for me to see that the paint is in the shape of a star, with a black candle at each point—like a ritual.

I don't notice that I've started picking at the skin along my cuticles until I feel a sharp stab of pain and look down to see blood pooling around another finger-nail. The cat's clouded gray eyes watch me, and the flies' constant buzz fills my ears.

"What are you doing?"

I whirl around, immediately spotting the dark-haired girl from the cafeteria—Riley. Her brown curls pool around her shoulders in perfect spirals, and her eyebrows start wide and taper to needle-thin points, as if they were drawn with a calligraphy pen. There isn't a single crease in her blue dress. It looks like she never sits down.

Riley looks past me, her pale blue eyes finding the skinned body of the cat. One of her eyebrows lifts, but her face remains otherwise unchanged.

"Gross." There's no inflection in her voice. She could be talking about the lasagna they served at lunch. I take a step away from the cat, nearly tripping over my sneakers.

"I didn't . . . I mean, that wasn't me. I didn't do that."

Riley turns her eyes on me. They're so pale they change her entire face, making her dark hair and brows seem severe. If I were going to paint her I'd have to use watercolors—only a drop of cerulean for her eyes, keeping them as light as possible.

"Of course you didn't." She glances down at the cat and shudders. "You're new, right? Sofia?"

"Yeah," I say, surprised she knows my name.

"Riley." She points to herself and her eyes grow several degrees warmer. "This is disgusting. I'm impressed you didn't hurl."

"Me, too." I wrinkle my nose. "Though I'm not sure I'm past the hurling stage yet."

"Right. Let's get out of here." Riley slides her arm around my shoulder and turns me away from the cat. "Come sit with me and my friends today."

She pulls me out from under the bleachers without waiting for an answer, which is probably a good thing because for once I don't know what to say. Girls I've known who look like Riley don't make friends with the new kid. It's a law of nature—Earth revolves around the sun, summer follows spring, and pretty, popular girls form cliques that are harder to break into than a bank vault. If attending seven schools in five years has taught me anything, that's it.

But Riley seemed genuine when she made her charity announcement in the cafeteria. Maybe she's different. Maybe Friend will live up to its name.

"We have the best spot for lunch," Riley explains. A few people smile and wave as we climb past them, and though Riley smiles back, she makes no move to stop and sit. "You can see everything that happens."

"Cool," I say. Riley steers us over to where only two other girls are sitting.

"Girls, this is Sofia. Sofia, this is Alexis." Riley points to a girl wearing all white—white skirt, white tank top, white sweater. Her pale blond hair is long enough for her to sit on, and she has a full, round face and wide eyes.

"Hey there," Alexis says, her voice carrying the hint of a Southern accent.

"And this is Grace." Riley motions to a girl with velvety chocolate skin and braided hair that she's twisted into a complicated-looking bun at the nape of her neck.

"Nice tie," I say, pointing to the polka-dot bow tie Grace is wearing as a necklace. Grace's lips part in a smile that's all teeth.

"Thanks! They're all the rage in Chicago."

"Grace is bringing culture to Mississippi," Alexis adds.

"Are you from Chicago?" I ask, sitting down on the bleachers next to them.

"My dad was transferred here two years ago," Grace says. "You ever been?"

I shake my head as Riley sits next to me and places her hands on her knees. Even her nails are perfect—trimmed and clean. I curl my hands into fists so she won't see my ragged cuticles.

"You'll never guess what Sof and I found under the bleachers."

*Sof.* The way Riley says my name is so personal and

friendly that I have to bite back a smile. Alexis and Grace lean forward, and Riley grins, a conspiratorial look on her face. She speaks in a whisper.

"A skinned dead cat."

"That's a joke, right?" Alexis asks, fumbling with the lace at the edge of her skirt. With her long hair and wide eyes, she looks like a Disney princess come to life.

Riley makes a cross over her heart. "Honest. I bet this is grounds for expulsion."

Grace shudders, nervously tapping a red Converse sneaker against the back of the bleacher in front of her. "They've got to at least suspend her. That's *disgusting*."

"Wait." I frown. "You know who killed that cat?"

Grace, Alexis, and Riley share a look I can't interpret. It's like they're trying to figure out if I can be trusted.

"You know that girl you were talking to in the cafeteria?" Riley asks, smoothing a curl behind one ear.

"Brooklyn?" I ask, surprised. I didn't realize Riley saw me talking to Brooklyn.

"Right. Brooklyn. She can be a little strange."

"Strange how?" I ask when Riley doesn't specify. Skinning a cat isn't strange. It's criminal.

Alexis scoots forward, and one of her knees bumps against mine. "There are rumors about Brooklyn," she says. "And since you're going to this school, you should probably know about them. They're intense."

"Rumors?"

"Last year she did a séance in the girls' locker room," Alexis continues. Her Southern accent gets heavier as she tells the story, and I get the feeling she's playing it up for effect. "I was in there the next day. The floor was all black—like it'd been burned—and the entire place smelled like sage."

"Or *something*," Grace adds, and Riley giggles.

"And earlier this year, a bunch of girls heard her chanting in the back of algebra class," Alexis finishes. "It's weird."

"Weird," I repeat. But that doesn't seem to cover it. Maybe the stories Alexis is telling are just rumors— but that cat was very real. And very dead. I shiver. In slightly different circumstances, I could be eating with Brooklyn right now, probably listening to terrible stories about Riley and her friends. I don't believe the same girl who offered me a Band-Aid would also kill a cat.

"And there's what happened last year," Riley adds, "with Mr. Willis . . ."

Before she can finish, a scream rolls off the football field. I jump up, jerking my head around to search for the screamer, but then the sound dissolves into laughter and fades away.

Just someone messing around. I sit back down, feeling stupid.

Grace leans forward and puts a hand on my knee. Her bow-tie necklace swings forward like a pendulum. "Guys, stop. We're scaring her."

"Sorry," Alexis says, wrinkling her nose. I look down at my hand. I've never liked scary stories. Even my grandmother's stories about Quetzalcoatl gave me nightmares. Absently, I rub the sketch of Quetzalcoatl, leaving behind a smudge of red. Blood from my thumb.

I look up and catch Riley watching me. Her eyes follow my finger as I run it over the lines of the serpent sketch on my hand. There's an odd look on her face, the same cold expression she wore when she first saw the dead cat behind the bleachers.

"It's just a stupid sketch." I lick one finger and try to rub it away, but I just smear the ink and blood into my skin. Riley shifts her eyes back to my face, her lips lifting at the corners. The effect isn't the same as it was behind the bleachers, when her smile made her face warmer. This smile doesn't reach Riley's eyes at all. They stay empty.

"Of course," she says.

# CHAPTER TWO

My classmates linger by the school doors after the last bell, waiting for rides from parents. You could walk down every street in Friend in an hour flat, but everyone still drives shiny black SUVs that leak air-conditioning and pop music from their open windows.

I see a flash of white out of the corner of my eye and turn in time to watch Alexis and Riley climb into a car. Grace waves at them from the sidewalk, surrounded by a circle of boys wearing sports jerseys and girls with shampoo-commercial hair. No matter the school, no matter the city, the popular group is always made of the same mix of athletes and the unfairly beautiful.

Everything in their lives is just a little shinier, richer—better. Of course I'd want that. Anyone would.

I slip past pockets of kids giggling and talking and start to walk home. I live so close that I can see my neighborhood from the school parking lot. The land here is all flat and dry, and the summers are so hot that I'm already sweating. It's the end of September and I'm still waiting for the last of the ninety-degree days to cool into autumn.

My neighborhood's entrance is marked by a four-foot-tall sign with the words HILL HOLLOW HOMES written in scrolling white letters. There's a fake waterfall and pond, though both are dry now, with weeds and dandelions growing through cracks in the sun-bleached rocks. Past that, the subdivision is a ghost town. The few dozen houses scattered across acres of bulldozed land are mostly empty.

I stare at the toes of my sneakers as I walk past three vacant lots and two identical houses, each with the same blue siding, white porch, and red front door as mine. Whoever chose the color scheme for our neighborhood was very patriotic.

Our place is the lone house on its block. It's a split-level with a narrow porch, a bay window, and a backyard that stretches for half an acre before the grass gives way to dirt and open land. The shed at the top of the driveway looks like a miniature version of the house itself, matching in color and style. Aside from the Uncle Sam paint job, it looks like every other house I've ever lived in.

I climb the rickety wooden steps to the door and let myself in, slipping on a brochure someone wedged under the front door. It's another advertisement for the Baptist church down the street. We've gotten two or three every day since we moved in. Mom hates the brochures so much she actually called the church to complain. She's always been a little touchy about religion. She never told me the whole story, just that Grandmother didn't take her getting pregnant out of wedlock very well.

I'm not a fan of anything that says I'm a mistake, either, but sometimes I wish she hadn't cut religion out of our lives so completely. Grandmother got over the unmarried thing by the time I was born, and I've always thought her dedication to Catholicism was beautiful. I stare down at the creepy bleeding heart on the front of the brochure. I should save them and make a collage of bleeding hearts for my wall. Mom would love that.

I drop my backpack on the kitchen table and grab a glass from the perfectly organized cupboard above the sink. We've only lived here a couple weeks, but almost all the boxes are already unpacked, our things carefully stored in cabinets and drawers. Sergeant Nina Flores handles everything with military precision.

I fill the glass with water and carry it to my grandmother's room down the hall. I knock softly before easing her door open.

"*Hola, Abuela,*" I greet her as I push her door closed with my elbow, blinking in the dark. Light hurts Grandmother's eyes, so we hung heavy curtains over the windows to block the sun and draped a scarf over her floor lamp to keep her room dim. The scarf turns the room red, and it takes a moment for my eyes to adjust.

I carefully make my way over to her bedside table and dig out the plastic container of her pills. Grandmother is sitting upright in bed, rosary beads clutched in her shaking hands. She stares ahead, lips moving wordlessly as she pushes the beads through her fingers.

She used to be beautiful, but it's hard to see that now. A few years ago, a stroke ruined the muscles on the right side of her body. Skin hangs from the bones in her face like melting wax, and her cheek droops so low that I can see the foggy white bottom half of her eye and the blood-red part inside her eyelid. The right side of her mouth is frozen in a twisted frown that doesn't match up with the smiling, laughing grandmother I remember.

I force myself to slip the pills past her cracked lips, then lift the water glass so she can take a drink. She's still the grandmother who sent me funny little poems written in Spanish on my birthday, I remind myself.

Water dribbles out of the right side of her mouth. I wipe it away with my sleeve, then squeeze her papery, soft hand. Her raspy breath interrupts the silence in the room, followed by the *click click* of the wooden rosary beads against the table attached to her hospital bed. She hasn't spoken a word since the stroke.

"Okay, exercise time," I say, setting the water glass down on her bedside table. I move her blanket and carefully stretch her right leg, then ease it upward to bend her knee so her muscles don't atrophy. I do this three times, just like her last nurse showed me. We haven't been able to find a nurse for her in Friend yet.

"You would love it here, you know," I say, putting her leg down. I slide the blanket back over it and move to the other leg. "They sell statues of the Virgin at the gas station."

Grandmother's rosary beads click against the table, like the second hand on a clock. She never really notices when I do her exercises. I'm not sure she can feel her legs anymore.

"And it's *hot* here." I grab her ankle and pull her left leg into a gentle stretch. "Do you remember that summer back in Mexico when it was so hot we tried to bake cookies on your windowsill?"

The *click*s of Grandmother's rosary beads are my only answer. I bite back the rest of my story, letting the question linger, unanswered, in the air between us. I picture Grandmother standing at the window, watching the cookies bubble in the heat. That was before the stroke, back when she was strong and beautiful. When she leaned forward, the thick gold cross she used to wear swung into the cookies and got covered in gooey batter. She gave me the cross and let me lick it off, like a spoon.

Now I slide her left leg back onto the bed and cover it with her blanket. Grandmother always said she'd give me that cross some day. She hasn't worn it since before her stroke.

I flip open the cardboard box on top of the stack next to her bed, which my mom marked CLOTHING & JEWELRY, and dig through piles of sundresses until I find Grandmother's jewelry box buried underneath. I open it to find a tangled ball of pearls and beads and thin silver chains. I pick through them, carefully separating the chunky gold cross.

"Beautiful," I murmur, slipping the cross over my head. "What do you think, Grandmother? You like?"

A line of drool spills from Grandmother's mouth. I drop my arm and wipe it away with my sleeve, cringing. Downstairs, the front door opens and closes. Footsteps creak in the foyer.

"Sofia?" my mom calls.

"See you later, *Abuela*," I whisper to Grandmother before slipping into the hall.

Mom stands in the kitchen with her back to me, a bag of groceries sitting on the counter next to her.

"My class was canceled, so I ran to the supermarket," she says when I walk in, putting a carton of milk in the fridge. Her green camo scrubs hang limply from her thin frame, and tiny spots of sweat dot the small of her back. "Do you know they sell Bibles next to the tabloids at the cash register?"

"The nerve," I say, playing along. Mom doesn't notice my sarcasm. She shakes her head and pushes the refrigerator door shut. I clear my throat. "So my first day was fine."

"What?" she asks, blinking at me. Her short black ponytail pulls at the skin around her face, making her confused expression seem more severe. Then her face relaxes as she remembers. "Right, your new school. Did you make any friends?"

She says this in such an upbeat, positive way that you'd think I meet dozens of friends every time we move to a new place. In reality, I'm lucky to find one or two people to hang out with for the few months we're there.

I study Mom's face for a moment to figure out if she's trying to be upbeat or if she's just oblivious. "Oh yeah. Hundreds," I say. "They're actually calling today Sofia Flores Day. Tomorrow I get a parade."

Mom opens her mouth—probably to tell me to watch my tone—but then her eyes drop to my neck. She points to the cross I'm still wearing.

"What's that?" she asks. Without waiting for me to explain, she holds out her hand.

There's no use arguing with her, so I slip the necklace over my head and place the cross in her open palm. "I thought it was pretty."

"It's not meant to be pretty." She sighs and puts the necklace in her pocket.

I press my lips together. Sometimes I wonder how it's possible that she and Grandmother are even related.

I head back to the kitchen table, unpacking my textbooks while Mom goes upstairs to return Grandmother's cross to her jewelry box. I finish my homework in silence.

But later that night, when I'm sure my mom's asleep, I sneak from my bed and creep, barefoot, into Grandmother's room. I slip the cross from the cardboard box. Grandmother stares ahead, unblinking, while I shove it into my backpack. Half of her mouth moves in the same slow, wordless prayer while the other half remains twisted, frozen.

The only sound I hear as I pull her bedroom door shut behind me is the *click click click* of her rosary beads echoing in the dark.

# CHAPTER THREE

The next day I wedge myself into one of the narrow green stalls in the girls' restroom between third and fourth periods. Black and silver Sharpie scrawls cover the door, telling me that Erika is a slut and that love that has been lost was never mine to begin with. A roll of toilet paper stretches across the black-and-white tile. As soon as I slide the lock into place, I hear the bathroom door creak open.

"Sofia?" The voice startles me, and I stand too fast, smacking my elbow on the plastic toilet paper holder. "Come out, come out, wherever you are."

"Riley?" My voice echoes off the bathroom walls. I

hadn't even looked for Riley and her friends this morning, assuming lunch was a one-time thing. They took pity on me and wanted to show me that Adams High wasn't all animal mutilation and satanic rituals. Still, I fumble with the lock and push the door open.

Riley leans over one of the sinks, adjusting the silk scarf tied around her neck. She looks like Audrey Hepburn in her sleeveless button-up shirt and high-waisted pants. The fluorescent light flickers overhead.

"Love the necklace," Riley says, catching my eye in the mirror as she pushes a perfect brown curl behind one ear. I touch the cross hanging from my neck.

"Thanks."

"We saw you come in," Alexis explains. She sets her white leather purse next to the dingy porcelain sink and digs out a tube of peach-colored lipstick. Her wispy blond hair trails over the counter as she paints her lips. "Thought we'd say hi."

Grace shuts the door, and Riley slides off one of her leather ballet flats and wedges it beneath the frame. She tests the door, but it doesn't budge.

"There. Now no one can surprise us."

I open my mouth to ask who's going to surprise us, then think of Brooklyn and the dead cat and close it again. Grace leans against the avocado-green counter. Today she's tucked her black braids behind a leopard-print headband, and she's wearing gold platform sandals that add an extra five inches to her height.

Riley puts her hands on my shoulders. "Sof, do you know how pretty you are?" she asks. "Guys, isn't Sofia pretty?"

"You're *so* pretty," Alexis purrs, capping her lipstick.

"Thanks," I say, studying their reflections in the mirror. Are they messing with me? My hair is shiny, and my skin can sometimes look golden in the sun, but these girls are perfect. Their skin looks dewy and fresh and completely poreless, even under the bathroom's harsh fluorescent lights, which are scientifically designed to make everyone look like a zombie.

I smile, shaking my head. Clearly they're just being nice.

Riley slides the hair tie off my ponytail and finger-combs my curls.

"Look how much better it is down," she says. She's right—it is better down, but I've been pulling it back so the Mississippi heat doesn't make it frizz. Already, a thin line of sweat forms on the back of my neck.

Alexis puts her lipstick back into her purse and removes a flask. I've never described a flask as cute before, but hers is tiny and silver, with flowers and vines engraved around the sides. She takes a swig and hands the flask to Grace.

"You guys drink?" I ask.

"We're taking Communion," Grace says. She closes her eyes and lifts the flask to her lips.

"Don't you go to church, Sof?" Riley frowns at my reflection, her fingers still tangled in my hair.

"My mom doesn't like church," I say. "But my grandmother's Catholic, so I know about Communion."

Alexis giggles and holds out her flask to me, but Grace snatches it from her hand before I can reach for it.

"Wait," she says. "Sofia can't have any. Remember? You two wouldn't even let me touch that flask until I was 'baptized in the blood of the lamb.'"

She says the last part with a thick Mississippi drawl. Alexis throws a wadded-up ball of toilet paper at her. "I don't sound like that," she says.

"Grace is right. You can't have Communion until you accept Jesus Christ as your personal Lord and Savior." Riley's voice is light, but there's a chill in her eyes. She wrinkles her nose at me.

"Right, my grandmother told me that," I say. Mom never let me get baptized, but I used to go to church with Grandmother all the time. When it was time to get Communion, the priest put his hand on my head and prayed for me instead of feeding me the host and wine.

When I look up again, Riley's staring at my reflection in the mirror. "You know, we could do it now, if you want. Baptize you."

I release a short laugh, positive she's joking. But Riley's face stays serious.

"You want to baptize me *here*?" I blurt out. "In the bathroom?"

"We have a sink," Riley says, shrugging. "And, Alexis, you know what to say, right?" Before Alexis can answer, Riley turns on the faucet and plugs up one of the sinks. Water pours into the stained white porcelain.

"But don't we need a priest for it to be real?" I ask.

Riley runs a finger along one of my curls. "It'll be real to us," she says. "Like becoming blood sisters. It's how we'll all know you're in the group."

I scratch at the skin along my cuticles and pretend to think this over. I had exactly one friend at my last school, and the coolest thing we ever did together was stay up late to watch reruns of *Saved by the Bell*.

"Let's do it," I say. Behind Riley, the sink fills. Water dribbles over the side and onto the tile floor. Grace leans past her and turns the faucet off.

"Careful," she says, but Riley doesn't seem to hear her. She grins at me, looking so giddy that I find myself smiling, too.

"Okay, cross your arms like this." Riley raises her arms in an *X* over her chest, Alexis's flask still gripped in one hand. I do the same. "Good," she says. "Now crouch down so you're over the sink. Alexis, you have to anoint her head with holy water."

"That's not holy water," Grace says. Riley tips Alexis's flask of wine over the water. A stream of red spills onto the surface, spreading like blood.

"The wine's been blessed," Riley says. "Same thing."

I let out a nervous giggle as Alexis dips a finger into the water. A blond eyelash clings to her cheek, making a tiny golden half-moon against her skin.

"Sofia, I baptize you in the name of the Father, the Son, and the Holy Spirit." She touches her finger to my forehead, chest, and both shoulders.

"Amen," Riley says. She places one hand at the base of my neck and the other over my crossed arms. I close my eyes and consider praying.

Before I can decide, Riley pushes my head into the sink.

The water hits my face like a slap. My eyes fly open, and on instinct I inhale, immediately flooding my lungs. I choke, releasing deep, hacking coughs that fill the water with bubbles and cloud my vision. I blink furiously, staring at the plugged-up drain at the bottom of the sink.

I try to lift my head, but Riley's hand is like a weight. I press my fingers into the edges of the sink. The bubbles in front of me turn spotty as my vision goes black. My fingers slacken as I start to lose consciousness when, finally, Riley removes her hand. I whip my head out of the water and gasp and cough. My hair hangs in front of my eyes in sopping-wet clumps.

Someone mops the hair out of my face. I blink and Riley's in front of me, her clear, pale eyes bright with excitement.

"Oh, Sof, are you okay? You did so well!"

"I think I survived," I gasp. Bursts of light still dot my periphery, but Riley's smile is sweet, genuine. She leans forward, kissing me on the cheek.

"Now you're one of us," she says. Her words spark something warm inside me. It flickers like a match. I'm one of them.

"Now you're saved," Riley says.

# CHAPTER FOUR

"**B**oo!"

I jump at the sudden voice, sending the pen I'd been sketching with sailing to the ground. Grace leaps up from behind the wooden bench I'm sitting on and doubles over in a fit of giggles.

"You're so easy to scare," she teases.

"Maybe you're just scary." I pick up my pen from the ground and throw it at her. When it bounces off her shoulder, Grace raises her hands in surrender.

"Hey! I come in peace. Riley asked me to find you."

"Oh, yeah?" Mom took Grandmother to a doctor's appointment today, so I don't have to race home right after school. All that's waiting for me are last night's leftovers. And Grace has a wicked glint in her eye. "What for?"

Grace straightens her leopard-print headband and perches on the bench next to me, staring at the basketball hoops in front of us. The outdoor basketball court is far less impressive than the football field. The concrete is all cracked and grungy, and there aren't even nets hanging from the hoops. The only other kids around the court are clichéd loiterers, sneaking cigarettes and passing around a gallon jug of generic-brand iced tea.

"We're headed to the house," Grace says. "Want to come?" Her fingernails are painted an electric blue that looks neon against her dark skin.

"Whose house?" I ask.

"Don't get your panties in a twist. You'll see." Grace winks. "And you'll *love* it."

I gather my pen and sketchbook and follow Grace away from school and through row after row of perfect suburban houses with Mississippi flags hanging from their porches. The extra-high platform sandals strapped to her already long, skinny legs make Grace move like a gazelle.

"This is what I love about small towns," she says as we walk. "Look at how safe and boring this whole neighborhood is. Back in Chicago, my dad would've called the police if I didn't come home right after school. But here?" Grace spreads her arms and spins in the street. "No one thinks we could get into trouble here. Can you taste the freedom, Sof?"

"Oh yeah," I say. "It tastes like—"

"Red wine," Grace interrupts. "And chocolate."

I laugh, jogging to keep up with her long strides. "I lived in DC for a couple of months freshman year. My friends and I skipped class once—just *one time*—and my teacher thought we'd been abducted." I decide not to mention that this was during my very brief Goth phase, and we skipped class to get fake IDs so we could see a band at a place called Club Trash. "The principal called the cops and everything."

"Nice!" Grace says, laughing. "You move around a lot, then? Are your parents military?"

"Army."

"Me, too," Grace says. "My dad's a combat engineer. We moved every two years of my life until he decided I needed an 'authentic high school experience.' Whatever that means."

I kick a rock with my sneaker and watch it skitter over the dusty sidewalk.

"And you like it here? The whole safe-and-boring thing never gets old?"

"Not if you're creative about it," Grace says with

another wicked smile. "Honestly, I didn't expect to like it here. When we first moved, some racist assholes at school used to make fun of my hair. But then I started hanging with Riley, and she made it clear that anyone who messed with me would pay." Grace shakes her head, like she still can't believe it. "When someone talked shit at my old school, you just kept quiet and hoped it stopped, you know?"

"Yeah," I say. I'm instantly hit with a memory from my last school of Lila Frank's high-pitched jackal laugh. "My old school was like that, too."

"Well, Riley doesn't stand for it. I'd walk through fire for that girl."

"What about Alexis?" I ask.

"She's a sweetheart. Practically Riley's double, though." Grace rolls her eyes. "It's kind of adorable, actually—you'll see."

Grace crosses a packed-dirt lot and ducks through a pocket of trees. A patchwork quilt of land unfolds around us. It's disturbingly empty, nothing but flattened dirt and twisting paved roads, all leading nowhere. The land is flat enough that I can see across the entire development, all the way to a far stretch of bare trees that were never cleared by the bulldozers.

I follow Grace down a block of vacant land and old construction sites. Two houses stand side by side where the road dead-ends. The first is unpainted, with heavy plastic tacked up where the windows and doors should be. When the wind blows, the plastic billows and collapses.

The second could be a completed house, except for the unfinished wood peeking through streaky white paint. Grace walks up the steps like she belongs there.

"Riley's dad's company owns this whole subdivision," she explains. "The land, the construction equipment—everything. Apparently, these houses never sold after the economy tanked, so now they just sit here taking up space. Since they technically belong to Riley's family, we borrow them from time to time."

I grin as I follow her up the stairs. An abandoned house surrounded by empty land definitely has the potential to be not boring. "I hear other teenagers have to hang out in their bedrooms."

"Poor teenagers," Grace says. She hesitates on the porch. "Almost forgot. Don't mention Josh unless Riley brings him up."

I frown, suddenly lost. "Wait, who?"

Grace pauses, her hand pressed against the door. "Josh is Riley's boyfriend. They got into this huge fight after lunch, and now Riley's all pissed at him. That's why we're doing this. Ri needed a girls' night."

"Got it—no Josh," I say.

Grace pushes the door open, and we make our way into the shadowy living room together. Afternoon light filters through the windows, but the cloudy blue plastic hanging over the glass keeps it dark. My eyes blur and I have to blink a few times before I can see. I hear fumbling and giggling in the darkness, then the sound of gas hissing to life, and the room fills with golden light. Alexis picks up a blue lantern and carries it over to us.

"Hey, Sof." She slips an arm around my shoulders to pull me into a hug. The sleeves of her lacy white shift dress scratch against my neck. "Ooh, I've been dying to get my hands on your hair," she says as she pulls away.

"Do *not* let her touch you!" Grace says. "Her idea of beauty is back-combing and Aqua Net."

Alexis pouts. "You make me sound trashy. Not all of us can pull off the color-blind diva look you've got going on."

"Hey, no need to take a swing at the ensemble," Grace says. I see Alexis's point. If anyone else tried on Grace's blue sequined skirt, leather jacket, and leopard-print headband they'd look like they got dressed in the dark. But Grace looks fierce.

"Where's Riley?" I ask, turning in place. Sleeping bags and pillows are scattered across the living room, and an upside-down milk crate acts as a side table, holding a Bible and an empty wine bottle. Cutouts of boys from magazines and postcards of old European churches cover the walls, along with hundreds of pictures of Riley, Alexis, and Grace.

I pull back the corner of a poster torn from a magazine and find a photograph of Riley and Alexis as little girls with long, skinny legs and goofy bows in their hair. They're dressed identically.

"Lexie and I have been friends forever," Riley says. I jump and whirl around—I didn't hear her come up behind me. She's barefoot and wearing a silky, kimono-style dress, her curls wild around her shoulders. It's like she got dressed up just for us. "You like our wall?"

"It's great," I say, my eyes moving over the pictures. Robert Pattinson's face peeks out from behind photo-booth snapshots, movie tickets, and stickers. I snicker. "*What* is this?"

"Grace had this huge crush on him for, like, a day," Alexis explains, stretching out on the floor. "But now she only has eyes for *Tom*."

"Shut *up*," Grace says, launching a pillow at Alexis. Alexis catches it and wedges it beneath her head.

"Ooh, who's Tom?" I ask, and Grace's cheeks redden.

"He's my boyfriend's older brother," Riley explains. "We all met when we were, like, seven."

Grace clears her throat.

"Excuse me," Riley says. "Everyone except for Grace.

The rest of us have been hanging at the lake since we were kids. See?"

Riley leans past me to smooth out a creased photograph of her and Alexis with two other guys all lounging in front of a huge house. It's a gray modern-looking house with steel-toned siding and gigantic floor-to-ceiling windows. Everything about the house looks sleek and intentional, from the Mercedes SUV parked out front to the perfectly trimmed leafy trees dotting the lawn and the long wooden dock artfully jutting out into a clear, still blue lake.

"This was at my family's house at Lake Whitney," she explains.

I lean in to look at the photograph. Alexis and Riley recline on the grass, tanned and gorgeous in their skimpy bikinis, their hair dried into beachy waves around their shoulders. Sitting between them is the cute boy from the cafeteria.

"Hey, I know him," I say, pointing to Charlie. He's wearing a damp white T-shirt over his swim trunks, and his messy hair is slicked away from his face, as if he just got out of the lake.

I turn back to Riley, but she isn't looking at Charlie. Her eyes are locked on the preppy boy next to him with a cleft chin and hair that hangs shaggily around his neck and forehead. The infamous Josh, I'm guessing.

Riley purses her lips and presses her finger over Josh's face, so I can only see his polo shirt.

"Big fight?" I ask. I know Grace told me not to mention it, but isn't that what tonight's about?

"Big enough that I either have to dump the jerk or somehow forget how pissed I am at him." Riley crosses the room, grabbing a half-full bottle of wine from behind a rolled-up sleeping bag. She waves it at me. "Guess which I chose."

"Forgetting by way of wine? I approve," I say.

"You know we've been together for three years?" she says. Riley yanks the cork out of the bottle. With her sexy dress and wild curls, she makes heartache look romantic. "We used to be so in love. Like Romeo and Juliet."

"Romeo and Juliet died at the end of that play, Ri," Grace points out. She crouches next to the milk crate and pulls out a bag of caramel corn and a plastic jar of Nutella. "Not a great sign."

"Whatever." Riley lifts the wine bottle to her mouth and drinks, deep. "This is just a blip. Josh and I are forever."

Grace hands me a spoon. "You eat it like this," she says. She unscrews the jar and dumps the caramel corn inside, then stirs the mixture with a spoon. "It tastes like heaven. Seriously."

I take a tentative bite. It's salty and sweet and crunchy at the same time. I dig another spoonful out of the jar. The corner of Riley's mouth hitches into a grin.

"So what's going on with you and Charlie?"

"What?" I stick another spoonful of Nutella and caramel corn in my mouth to cover my embarrassment. "There's no me and Charlie," I say, swallowing.

"Oh please. I saw the way you undressed his photo with your eyes." Riley collapses onto a pile of pillows and lifts the wine bottle to her mouth again. "You *want* him."

"Does Sofia have a crush already?" Alexis asks.

"It's not a crush," I insist, heat creeping up my neck with every word. "I just . . .like his arms."

Alexis falls back onto the pillows, laughing, and Grace makes kissy noises at me as I hand over the spoon and Nutella.

"My, what fabulous taste you have. Charlie's a ten." Riley smoothes her dress down over her thighs. "I could probably make that happen for you. If you wanted."

"Make that happen?" I say. "We're not dogs. You can't throw us in a room and hope we mate."

"Can't I?" Riley fixes those pale blue eyes on me, and I immediately realize how wrong I am. Riley clearly gets whatever she wants, no matter how insane it sounds.

"Wait a second," Grace says. "How come I never got this offer with Tom?"

"Tom doesn't know what the hell he wants, Gray. You could do so much better. But Charlie . . . Charlie I could work with."

Riley pushes herself to her knees and leans forward, brushing the back of her hand against my cheek. "And just look at Sofia. Isn't she completely gorgeous? She was made to have someone fall insanely in love with her."

My skin tingles where Riley touches it. Her words spark something inside me. I picture Charlie sliding an arm around my shoulders and pulling me close. I feel the heat of his lips against mine, and my body tightens with want. My past boyfriends have always been more of the fumble-around-in-the-dark variety. There was never any talk of love.

I shake my head, suddenly embarrassed. "I'm confused—I thought Charlie was friends with Brooklyn."

Riley frowns, staring at me over the top of the wine bottle. "Why would you think that?"

"No reason, really. He just said hi to her in the lunch line yesterday."

Alexis's lips move as she counts the kernels of popcorn in her hand. "That boy is too nice for his own good," she mutters.

"We all used to be friends, you know," Riley says. "Brooklyn, too."

"I would once again like to point out that this was

BG," Grace says. "Before Grace. Otherwise known as the Dark Ages."

"It's also before Brooklyn started dressing like an Urban Outfitters catalog," Riley adds, fingering the hem of her dress. "She used to be really sweet, but once we started high school, she just . . . changed."

I think of the way Brooklyn narrowed her eyes at Riley in the cafeteria, aiming an imaginary gun at her head. "Why?"

"No one knows." Riley spins the wine bottle with her fingertips, leaving a red ring behind on the floor. She picks it up and passes it to Alexis. "Sometimes I wonder if it's a cry for help. Like maybe God wants us to save her. But we've all tried to talk to her, and she won't listen. I think there's just too much history between us."

"She was even horrible to Grace," Alexis says, passing me the wine bottle. "And she barely knows her."

"She was okay to me," I say. I let the wine roll over my tongue, holding it in my mouth.

"Really?" Grace asks.

I shrug. "I mean, we didn't paint each other's nails or anything, but she gave me a Band-Aid."

Alexis snickers. "Can you imagine doing your nails with Brooklyn? I bet every bottle of polish she owns is black."

Alexis giggles even harder, but Riley suddenly sits up straight.

"Wait a second. Maybe you *should*," she says. There's a manic, excited light in her pale eyes—and she's aiming them right at me. "Hang out with Brooklyn, I mean. I don't think she's seen you with us yet. You can find out why she's such a bitch now."

"You want me to spy on her?" I ask.

"Come on, Ri, don't ask her to do that." Grace throws a piece of popcorn at Riley. "It's weird."

"I guess it does sound like spying." Riley's shoulders slump. "Sorry, Sof, I didn't mean it like that. I was just thinking it'd be cool if we could help her."

"Right, of course," I say, but the idea sticks in my head. I chose Riley and her friends over Brooklyn, and I definitely prefer Nutella and red wine over animal mutilation and locker room séances. Still, I wonder what Brooklyn's really like.

Suddenly, Alexis sits up, dropping the rest of her caramel corn on the floor.

"Guys, let's do something else," she says, wiping the popcorn dust coating her fingers onto one of the sleeping bags. "Sofia's going to think that all we do is sit around and gossip about Brooklyn."

"Speak for yourself," Grace says. "I barely even knew that psycho."

"Hand me that." Alexis points to the wine bottle I'm still holding, and I pass it to her. She takes a deep drink.

"Okay, so this is a game Ri and I used to play all the time when we were kids. It's called *concentration*."

"Ugh! No." Riley groans, making a face. "That game is so stupid, Lexie."

"Shut up. It's perfect," Alexis says. "Come on, Grace. I'll do you first."

Grace crawls over to Alexis and sits in front of her, clenching her eyes shut. Alexis knocks on the top of her head, then slides her fingers over the back of her neck and shoulders. Grace snickers.

"After I finish speaking, you will be put into a trance," Alexis continues, walking her fingers up and down Grace's spine. "This trance will allow you to see the most important moment of your life, past or present."

"Oh, god," I groan. Riley laughs through her clenched lips.

"Shut up," Alexis says. "This is totally scientific."

"Ignore them. I'm ready," Grace says.

"Good. Now concentrate," Alexis whispers. She knife-chops her hands against Grace's back and kneads her fingers against her neck and shoulders. Grace's head drops in relaxation, and her eyes close. "What do you see?"

"I see . . ." Grace sways back in forth. Her eyelids flicker, and her lips part in a faint smile. "I see a beach. It's long and white. Stretched out in front of it is the most beautiful, sparkling blue ocean."

"Good," Alexis whispers. "What else?"

Grace's smile fades. "I'm not alone," she says. There's a chill in her voice now. I shiver. "There's someone there. Someone I can't see."

"Turn around," Alexis says. Grace nods. She stops swaying, and her whole body goes rigid. "Look at who's standing behind you, Grace. Now . . . describe him to me."

Grace's eyes shoot open.

"It's Tom," she says, wiggling her eyebrows. "He's spread out across a beach towel, shirtless. He wants to help rub suntan lotion on my back."

Alexis smacks Grace on the arm, and Grace snorts with laughter. "Loser," Alexis says, smiling. "Okay, who's next? Riley?"

Riley takes another drink of wine, shaking her head. "No way. I'm protesting."

Alexis rolls her eyes. "Sofia, then. Come on."

"Fine," I say, cracking a smile. I slide over to Alexis, and she sits up on her knees, putting her hands on my arms. She digs her knuckles into my shoulders, then drags her fingers down my back.

"Concentrate," she whispers as I close my eyes. "Listen to the sound of my voice. . . ."

With my eyes closed, I notice how warm it is in this room. Heat hovers around my skin and presses against my arms. I sway a little, then release a bubbling giggle.

I'm a lightweight—the wine has already made me drunk.

Alexis's fingers dig into my back, and I try not to laugh again. It tickles. The other girls have gone silent. I want to open my eyes and see what they're doing, but my eyelids are so heavy. My mind spins. Jesus, how much wine did I have? I'm starting to feel dizzy. . . .

"Concentrate," Alexis repeats, and to my surprise something does flicker against my eyelids. It's a memory from my old school.

"Tell me what you see," Alexis says.

*A sharp elbow jams into my side, and I stumble into a row of puke-green lockers. My books fall from my arms and slap against the floor.*

*Whoever elbowed me snickers as he continues down the hallway. I drop to my knees to gather my things, not bothering to lift my head.*

*"Let me help you." Karen kneels to pick up my books. Karen is barely five feet tall, with bobbed blond hair and freckles— the kind of cute-pretty that makes her less likely to be a total bitch, unlike all the other cheerleaders at this school. Even so, I'm sure she wouldn't talk to me at all if we weren't lab partners in biology.*

*She hands me my textbook. "You excited?" she asks as we walk into class and slide onto the rickety wooden stools next to our lab table. "The big experiment is today."*

*I roll my eyes. All week, our bio teacher, Mr. Baer, has been talking about our class "experiment" like it's this huge event. Really, we'll just be swiping the countertops and trash cans with Q-tips to see if we can collect some germs to grow in a petri dish. "Oh yeah. I'm so excited."*

*Karen laughs. "Where do you think we'll find the most germs?" she asks. She narrows her eyes as she looks around the room, settling on Mr. Baer. "How about the gap between Mr. Baer's teeth?"*

*"Ew! You're probably right. His coffee breath is bad enough to take out a village."*

*Lila swivels around on her stool, leaning her back against the lab table directly in front of us. Karen chokes back the rest of her laughter.*

*"What are you laughing at, Greasy?" Lila asks. Lila's a senior, a varsity cheerleader, and so far out of my social circle that the only time I see her outside of class is when she's on top of the human pyramid at pep rallies.*

*My cheeks burn and I duck my head, letting my hair swing forward to cover my blushing face. I got the nickname Greasy a couple of months ago, when some JV cheerleader in my English class said it looked like I never washed my hair. I wash my hair every day, but my mom's been on this all-natural kick lately. The shampoo she buys is made from avocados, and it weighs my hair down, making it look shiny and clumpy.*

*"Careful, Karen," Lila's lab partner, Erin, says without*

*turning around on her stool. She brushes her own perfect brunette waves back behind one ear. "Get close enough to Greasy and you're going to catch whatever she has."*

*"Right," Karen says, but when Lila turns back around she glances back at me. "Ignore them," she whispers. She says it quietly, though, and she shoots a glance at Lila and Erin, obviously hoping they don't hear.*

"Sof? Sofia, can you hear us?"

I open my eyes. Riley, Alexis, and Grace are all staring at me. My cheeks burn with embarrassment and I blink, trying to remember the last thing Alexis said.

"Well?" Grace asks. "What did you see?"

I roll my lower lip between my teeth, the memory still fresh in my head.

Riley gives me a quizzical look. "Are you okay, Sof?" she asks. "Did you really see something?"

"Yes," I say. Then I grab a stray piece of popcorn from the floor and throw it at Grace. "I saw Tom. He said you should apply your own sunscreen."

Alexis hoots with laughter. Riley takes the Nutella from her and licks the back of the spoon. She catches my eye and winks. "Looks like Sofia fits in better than we thought."

# CHAPTER FIVE

"How did you all like *The Divine Comedy*?" Ms. Carey asks our English lit class the next day. I stare down at my notebook, doodling in the margins. I hate class discussions, and being tired and a little hungover from last night doesn't help. It feels as if someone's pressing my eyes closed—I have to fight to keep them open.

"Isn't this book about Satan?" asks some blond girl I've never talked to before. "Should we be reading about Satan at school?"

I deepen the familiar lines of Quetzalcoatl's feathered tail with my pen. That sounds like something Riley would say. Ms. Carey nods.

"That's a good point, Angela. Can anyone tell me why we'd read *The Divine Comedy* in high school?"

No one answers. Ms. Carey taps a leather loafer on the floor.

"Come on, guys, there are no wrong answers here. What do you think? Why are we reading *this* book?"

"Because high school is hell."

I stop sketching and glance over my shoulder. Brooklyn sits in the back corner next to the windows. Usually she spends class with her head on her desk, but today she's staring at Ms. Carey, defiant. She stretches the chain that hangs from her neck between two fingers, and the gold ring swings from side to side, like a pendulum.

"If we have to live it, we may as well read about it," she adds.

"Well, that was more colorfully put than I'd have liked," Ms. Carey says as the students around us snicker. I stop doodling and my pen bleeds ink onto the page.

In the back row, Brooklyn flicks her own paperback copy of the book with one finger, sending it sliding over her desk and onto the floor. I shake my head, a little impressed. She really doesn't care what anyone around her thinks. Must be nice.

Before Ms. Carey can comment further, the bell rings and the rest of the students start gathering their things.

Brooklyn winds her way through the chairs and desks. She walks past me without a word.

Making a quick decision, I shove my notebook into my bag and drop behind her as she makes her way down the hall. Riley didn't mention the spying thing again, and by this morning I'm pretty sure everyone forgot about it. But I keep wondering about Brooklyn, if she's really into séances and chanting and animal mutilation, or if it's all just rumors. And my biggest question: If she really was friends with Riley, why would she throw that away?

"Hey," I say. When Brooklyn doesn't turn around, I jog up next to her. "That was funny—what you said about high school being like hell."

"Was it?" Brooklyn shuffles through her bag, pulling out a pack of cigarettes. The entire box is covered in black Sharpie scribbles, so you can't even see the brand name. Brooklyn slides a cigarette from the pack and puts it in her mouth, unlit. We aren't even out of school yet.

"Are you doing anything now?" My lame attempt at being laid-back makes me cringe. Brooklyn stops walking in the middle of the hallway, forcing the kids behind us to move around her.

"Aren't you one of Riley's?"

"What does that mean?"

"That she's collected you." Brooklyn fumbles with the gold ring at her neck, sliding it on and off one of her fingers. "Riley likes new girls. She takes it upon herself to 'befriend the friendless.'"

"I can't hang out with both of you?" I ask.

Brooklyn shrugs and starts walking again. "Do what you want."

It isn't exactly an invitation, but I follow her out the school doors and over to the bike rack anyway.

"What's with the ring?" I ask, nodding at her necklace. Brooklyn grins.

"Souvenir from one of my lovers." She holds the ring up to the light so I see the engraving on the inside: CARLTON & JULIANNA 1979.

I wrinkle my nose. "That's sick," I say. Brooklyn just laughs.

Even before we reach the bike rack, I can tell which is hers—the vintage eighties one with the handlebars that curl around the rider's hands. Brooklyn painted it bright pink with flecks of black, so it looks like a watermelon, and the handlebars and seat are covered in peeling green duct tape.

I stand awkwardly next to her while she unlocks her bike, then loops the thick chain around her arm and starts to push it away.

"I've got an appointment," Brooklyn says. The cigarette, still unlit, dangles from her lips. "Tag along if you like."

I hesitate, but curiosity gets the better of me. "Sure." I pull my bag over my shoulder and trail after her as she wheels her bike through the parking lot, toward a sidewalk that leads in the direction opposite my neighborhood. When she isn't looking, I pull my cell phone out to check the time. Grandmother will be fine if I'm a half an hour late.

Brooklyn takes me to an old service road past the main street into town. We pass a dive bar and an alley leading to an empty parking lot. Brooklyn stops at a tiny tattoo parlor and starts to lock up her bike.

"This is where your appointment is?" I squint through the dirty windows. I can just make out the hazy shapes of a counter and plastic chairs.

"'Appointment' might be stretching it." Brooklyn takes the cigarette she never did get around to smoking out of her mouth and sticks it behind one ear. Then she leans against the door of the tattoo parlor to push it open. It smells like smoke inside, and some sort of lemon-scented disinfectant. Brooklyn walks up to the counter and slides her elbows over the dingy vinyl.

"Ollie! You here?" she shouts. She leans over the counter like she's trying to see into the back room. I take the rest of the shop in. The walls are covered with hand-drawn illustrations of rose and skull tattoos, with nude *Playboy* centerfolds taped between them. Classy.

"Hey, new girl!"

The voice comes from behind me and I jump, nearly tripping over my own feet as I spin around. Charlie is sitting cross-legged on the cracked plastic couch, a textbook propped open on his knees. In his rumpled polo and faded jeans, he looks as out of place here as I do.

"It's Sofia, actually." A blush creeps up my neck. "What are you doing here?"

"Homework." He motions to the textbook on his lap and smiles. A dimple appears in his cheek, and for a second I can't help but stare. His eyes shift behind me.

"Hey, Brooklyn," he says with a nod.

"Charlie-boy," Brooklyn says. "Your brother around?"

"Yeah. Don't think he's going to be happy to see you, though. He's got a customer at four."

"We'll see about that." Brooklyn shifts her weight to her arms, hoists herself onto the counter, and scoots across.

"Hey." Charlie pushes aside his textbook and stands as Brooklyn slides off the other side of the counter. "You know we have a door, right?"

"Doors are for suckers." Brooklyn sticks out her tongue and disappears into the back of the shop. I hesitate, not sure if I should follow her.

"Here." Charlie unlatches a gate in the display case, swinging it open for me. "See? We're not all heathens."

"Thanks," I say. Giving him one last shy smile, I make my way to the back to find Brooklyn.

The tattoo parlor is cleaner than I expected. The green-and-white vinyl floors are cracked and peeling, but it looks as if they've been mopped recently. The entire room has a worn-in, laid-back vibe that actually feels kind of homey. Like a familiar booth at your favorite cheesy diner.

Red plastic chairs are scattered across the room, all covered in duct tape, with metal trays set up next to them. Brooklyn leans against one of the chairs, talking to an older version of Charlie—a guy who's tall and thin, with dark eyes. A thorny rose tattoo stretches across his neck, and three thick metal piercings jut out from his each of his ears like nails.

"Come on, Ollie," Brooklyn's saying as I approach. Ollie shakes his head.

"Look, I don't have time today."

Brooklyn peels a strip of duct tape off the chair. "Santos isn't here. You can just let me use his equipment. I think I could do it myself."

"You kidding? You're sixteen."

Brooklyn smiles, so wide I could count all her teeth if I wanted to. "That never stopped you before."

The bell above the door out front jingles. I glance over my shoulder as a college girl in a jean skirt and Uggs walks in, her hair pulled into a high ponytail. Out front, Charlie says something to her about Ollie being out in a minute.

Ollie's considering Brooklyn now, like he's trying to decide if she'll cause more trouble out front with his customer or back with his needles. He comes to the same conclusion I do.

"Just wait for me back here," he says. "I'll try to fit you in later."

Brooklyn folds her hands over her chest, fluttering her eyelashes. "My hero." Ollie groans and heads back out front while Brooklyn leans against a chair half hidden by a curtain off to the left. Dozens of identical black stickers cover the chair, the words SANTOS AND THE RAISONETTES printed on all of them.

"Santos's band," Brooklyn says, nodding at the stickers. "Isn't that the worst band name you ever heard?"

"How do you even know these people?" I ask, sitting down in the chair. Brooklyn grabs a bar stool and pulls it up next to me.

"I used to work here," she says. "I had a fake license, and Ollie let me apprentice with him until Charlie ratted me out and told him I was only sixteen."

"You've given people tattoos?"

"Nah, I did mostly piercings. See this one?" Brooklyn pushes back her hair to show me a large safety pin running from her cartilage to her earlobe.

"Did that myself," she says proudly. "You got anything pierced?" I shake my head. Brooklyn's mouth drops open. "Not even ears?"

"My mom doesn't like piercings," I say.

"And you . . . what? Just let her make those decisions for you?"

"What are you going to get tattooed?" I ask to change the subject.

"Dunno yet," Brooklyn says. "I was thinking of that snake thing you had on your hand a couple of days ago. That was pretty cool."

"Quetzalcoatl?"

"Is that what it's called?" Brooklyn asks. "You think you could draw it for Ollie?"

"Sure. If you want me to." I'm flattered, and my fingers itch to reach for my pen. Brooklyn narrows her eyes at me.

"You know, you'd look wicked cool with an eyebrow ring."

"You think so?" Almost unconsciously, I lift a finger to my eyebrow. Then, thinking of my mom's reaction, I push the thought away. There was a time I would have done it just to get a reaction from her, but it's not worth it now, not when things are going so well.

"Is it because of your little friends?" Brooklyn snickers, staring down at the tray next to her. It's covered in needles, tiny hoop earrings, ointments, and, inexplicably, a cucumber-melon-scented candle from Bath & Body Works. "I bet they think piercings are a *sin*. God, I don't know how you can stand the holier-than-thou crew."

"I thought you all used to be friends," I say. Brooklyn slides a needle off the metal table and holds it between two fingers.

"You've been talking about me?" she asks. I shift my eyes away from the needle. It's thick—thicker than I expected it to be.

"They just said you used to hang out with them, and that you changed," I say.

Brooklyn shrugs, turning the needle in her fingers. "Let's just say that after years of worshipping at the altar of Riley, I decided I wanted to have some *fun*." The fluorescent light buzzes overhead, casting a flickering yellow glow across the needle's surface. "Be honest now, Sofia. Do you really want to spend high school praying? Because you look like someone who knows how to have fun."

I think of my Goth friends showing their fake IDs to the bouncer at Club Trash, or my last boyfriend—if you could even call him that—who was more interested in his bong than in me. Last night, with Riley, Grace, and Alexis, I finally felt like I belonged.

Still, sitting here with Brooklyn fits, too. The duct-tape-covered vinyl and indie rock blasting from the iPod in the corner remind me of dozens of nights in smoky basements. I lift my eyes to meet Brooklyn's, and a rush of adrenaline spreads through me, like warmth uncurling beneath my skin. I can't help imagining her threading that needle through my eyebrow, the bright pain as it tears through my skin.

"Come on," she urges, touching the needle to my eyebrow. "I dare you."

"No." I shake my head. "I really can't."

"It wouldn't be forever," Brooklyn says. "You can take the ring out whenever you want, and your mom wouldn't even know you had it."

I stare down at the rings, imagining how cool it'd be to have a secret piercing, to get away with this right under my mom's nose. I could even hide it from Riley and the others, if I wanted. I begin to smile.

"Jesus." Brooklyn hops on her stool, then curls a hand beneath the seat, like she's forcing herself to stay put. "You *have* to."

I laugh, and her voice echoes in my head. *I dare you.* I lean forward, and the soaring, whooping feeling of adrenaline rises in my chest. I don't want it to go away.

"Fine. Do it," I say.

Brooklyn grins, the same wolfish grin that shows all her teeth. She sets the needle back down on the tray and picks up a cotton swab and a bottle without a label.

"Eyebrow, right?" she asks, squirting clear liquid onto the swab. I nod, and she leans forward and dabs at my face. "This is just antiseptic. It'll keep you from getting an infection."

"Okay," I say. Brooklyn tosses the cotton aside and picks up the needle again.

"Keep still or it'll be crooked."

I take a deep breath and hold it, digging my teeth into my lower lip. Brooklyn moves in close to me, and I stare at her eyes to keep from looking at the needle. They're dark brown, almost black. I can barely see the outline of her pupil.

I swear I feel the needle a second before Brooklyn slides it through my skin. It's nothing like the sharp, sudden prick I'd been imagining. This pain is slow. Nausea floods my stomach, and I have to close my eyes to keep from feeling dizzy.

"*Shit*," I hiss, letting out my breath in a rush. There's a pop, and I feel the needle slide through the other side of my eyebrow.

I wrap my hand around the chair's armrest and force myself to breathe as the room around me spins. I feel strangely hot. It's so hot that I'm sweating, and now the floor is rising and falling beneath me. I blink, and it's as if I'm looking through a camera's fish-eye lens. Brooklyn is close, but everything around her is distorted and far away.

"Are you okay?" Brooklyn's forehead creases in concern. I stare at my knees, trying to focus on breathing.

When I look up again, Brooklyn straddles her stool and we're sitting so close that our knees touch. She holds the needle in front of her, and my blood winds down the side. The overhead light flickers—it's reflected in Brooklyn's black eyes and in the red droplet of my blood.

"Sofia," Brooklyn says. She slides the needle into her mouth, smearing her lips with red blood. "Now you're reborn," she says, her voice distorted, like I'm hearing it underwater. The light flickers again, and everything goes black.

\* \* \*

The next thing I'm aware of is a weight pressing against my eyelids. My throat is dry and scratchy, and I try to speak, but the sound that escapes my mouth is strangled, like a gasp. I force my eyes open, and light fractures and breaks in front of me, making me squint.

"Hey, Sleeping Beauty. How you feeling?"

"Brooklyn?" I blink and, slowly, my vision clears. I'm not in the tattoo parlor chair anymore. I'm lying in some sort of office area, and Brooklyn is perched on the edge of a desk in front of me. Her shirtsleeve is rolled up, exposing a freshly bandaged shoulder. She removes a cigarette from her mouth and blows out a plume of smoke that curls around her.

"You passed out," she explains. "My cousin's like that—he'd pass out from a paper cut. Charlie and Ollie moved you so you wouldn't freak out the other customers."

"Charlie moved me?" I ask, feeling an immediate pang of embarrassment. Brooklyn nods. There's no blood on her mouth. No strange glinting light in her black eyes or manic smile. It was a dream. Or a hallucination, maybe.

"What time is it?"

Brooklyn pulls a cell phone out of her pocket and squints down at it. "Quarter after six."

"Crap." I sit up, trying to ignore the headache beating at my temples. The office door opens, and Charlie appears, holding a bottle of water. I grab my backpack and stand. The room spins, and I hold on to the desk to steady myself.

"Feeling better?" he asks. He smiles, and the spinning immediately gets worse.

"Where's the fire?" Brooklyn asks, lifting the cigarette back to her mouth.

"I just need to get home. Thanks for the—" I motion to my eyebrow, then duck past Charlie and out of the office, cheeks burning in embarrassment.

As soon as I'm outside, I start to run. My backpack digs painfully into my shoulder and slaps against my hip as I move. If my mom gets home before I do and finds out I left Grandmother alone, I'm screwed. I try to do the math in my head—it takes me about five minutes to walk home from school, and Brooklyn and I walked for maybe ten minutes to get to the tattoo parlor. Tonight my mom's class ends at six thirty, and she'll be home by six forty-five. As long as I don't get lost, I should be fine.

My chest burns, and my breath escapes in ragged gasps. I barely notice the buildings and houses as I race past them, working and reworking the math in my head. I'm almost home. I'm fine. I'll be fine.

I tear up the driveway to our house and fit my key into the lock, glancing at the clock in the hallway once I'm inside: 6:40. I close my eyes, lean against the front door, and breathe. I made it.

Kicking off my shoes, I head down the hall and duck into the bathroom across from Grandmother's bedroom. Her door is open, and the red-tinted lamplight spills into the hall. I hear her wheezing breaths and the rosary beads clicking against her table as I walk past.

"You okay, *Abuela*?" I call to her as I shrug off my backpack and set it on the toilet seat. Then I catch sight of myself in the mirror over the sink.

The tiny gold hoop circles the narrowest part of my eyebrow, looking foreign and wrong against my dark skin. I lean in to touch it, cringing when my finger brushes against the purple bruise spreading across my skin.

I glance over my shoulder into Grandmother's room.
She's sitting up in bed, her dark eyes staring out at me
from the shadows of her red-tinted room. Her lips mouth
wordless prayers as she counts the beads on her rosary.

My breath is shallow, fast. I turn back around, wrapping my fingers around the cold porcelain sink to try to
calm myself down. My reflection stares back at me, the
tiny golden hoop twinkling above my right eye.

Mom's car rumbles into the driveway, and the engine
cuts. In the quiet that follows, I swear I hear my heart
beating against my chest. I don't think. I lean in close to
the mirror, so close I could count the number of lashes
on my eyelid. I hold the tiny golden hoop steady with
two fingers and twist the bead off. Then I rock the hoop
back and forth, ignoring the blistering pain as I ease it
out of my skin. Blood bubbles beneath my fingers.

Grandmother watches me from her bedroom. The front
door opens and slams closed. Footsteps thud in the foyer.

"Sofia?"

I let the golden hoop fall from my fingers, and it
clinks against the sink, landing a half an inch from the
drain. I switch on the faucet and it swirls down the drain
in a whirlpool of pink, bloodstained water. Only once it's
gone do I allow myself to breathe again.

"I'm in the bathroom, Mom," I call. I rinse my hands
and look back up at the mirror. The blood is still leaking

from the hole in my eyebrow. It's smudged across my forehead and cheek, crusted into my eyelashes. I unwind a length of toilet paper from the roll and bunch it up into a ball, holding it to my face.

Beneath my fingers, the blood blossoms like a flower. Within seconds, the entire tissue is stained red.

# CHAPTER SIX

"I still don't understand why it would bleed so much." Mom wraps up the chicken we just had for dinner in tinfoil while I fill the sink with soapy water and start the dishes. I shrug, staring at a folded dishtowel next to the sink. It's red and white with a picture of a rooster on it.

"It was a really big zit," I say. I cleaned the blood from my face and covered the piercing with a Band-Aid before my mom saw it, but I've had to change the Band-Aid twice since she's been home. Already the new one is red with blood.

Mom puts the chicken in the fridge, frowning as she closes the door. Our phone rings, and Mom leans over the counter and picks it up. "Flores residence," she answers. A tinny-sounding voice echoes from the other end of the receiver, and Mom smiles. "One moment. It's your friend Riley," she says, handing me the phone. "She says she has a homework question. Just don't take too long."

I slip out the back door with the phone and curl up in the wooden chair on our patio. Our backyard stretches forever, without any streetlights or nearby houses to break it up. It's unnerving, like being walled in on all sides with empty space. Insects buzz restlessly, like white noise. I tuck my legs beneath me.

"Riley?" I say into the phone.

"Sof? I saw you with Brooklyn!" My stomach twists, but Riley continues talking before I can worry about whether she changed her mind about the spying. "Why didn't you tell me? What did you find out?"

"Nothing, really. She took me with her to get a tattoo." I run a finger along the edge of the bandage on my forehead but decide to keep the details of my piercing to myself.

"That's it?" Riley sounds disappointed. I lower my hand, quiet for a second as I try to work out what I want to say.

"What did you expect me to find?" My voice comes out sharper than I intend, but I don't apologize for it.

Riley said she was trying to help Brooklyn, but it sounds like she just wanted her to screw up.

"She skinned a cat and left it outside our school." Riley's voice has an edge to it. "Or did you forget?"

I press my lips together to keep myself from arguing. Riley *thinks* Brooklyn skinned that cat. Tattoos and cigarettes aren't in the same league as animal mutilation.

Riley clears her throat.

"Are you okay, Sof? She didn't hurt you, did she? Or manipulate you in some way?" The concern in Riley's voice is real, and suddenly I feel terrible. *Riley's* been a real friend to me since I got here, not Brooklyn. I exhale and shake my head, pulling at a piece of loose skin near my fingernail.

"No, it was nothing like that. She was . . ." *Cool.* The word pops into my head uninvited. "She was weird," I finish instead.

As the word leaves my mouth I realize it's just as true. Brooklyn was cool, but I get what Riley means— something about her did feel off. I think of her slender fingers on Santos's needles, her wolfish grin, and how she persuaded me so effortlessly to get a piercing. She made it too easy to be bad.

"Maybe I'll find something better tomorrow," I mumble. There's a beat of silence. I clear my throat. "How are things between you and Josh?"

"Oh, didn't you hear? We're all better now," Riley says. "He sent flowers to my class third period. Roses."

"Wow. That's great."

"Listen," Riley says before I can continue. "I just want to say I'm sorry if I made you uncomfortable when I asked you to hang out with Brooklyn."

"Riley, you didn't," I insist. "Really."

"It's just that I think she really needs help. I have this feeling like she's standing on the edge of a cliff and she's about to go over. Like she'll fall if we don't help her."

I run my thumb over a cuticle in slow circles. I try to picture Brooklyn at the edge of a cliff, her combat boots sending rocks off the edge, but it just doesn't fit with the girl I hung out with this afternoon. Brooklyn was having fun, not crying out for help. "You really think it's that bad?"

"I *really* do. Did she tell you she's having a party tomorrow?"

"She didn't mention it."

"Well, I heard some kids talking about it at school. It's supposed to be intense. You should go."

I run my tongue over my lips, which are dry now from the cold creeping over the yard. The last party I went to was in a house in the woods, next to the train tracks that ran through town. A bunch of football players stood just inside the door, loudly rating every girl who walked past, and every time a train rolled through, the whole house shook and everyone took a shot.

When I don't answer right away, Riley starts to plead. "Come on, Sofia! There's a reason I picked you for this. Some people have evil inside them, but *that's* what God is for, to fix them when they can't fix themselves. We can still fix Brooklyn."

The insects in the yard have gone still, but wind sweeps over the grass and pounds against the windows. I shiver and pull my arms around my chest. Grandmother used to pray for people in her neighborhood when she thought they needed strength. This isn't any different, I guess. Riley's just a little more active with her faith. Grams would probably like her.

"Sof? Are you still there?"

"Yeah," I say. "I'll do it. Promise."

* * *

I shiver as I make my way to Brooklyn's for the party the next night. An owl hoots in a nearby tree. I pull my sweatshirt tighter around my shoulders and lower my face. Wind sweeps through the tree branches, rattling them like bones. A man with a sagging gut and pock-marked face winks at me.

"How you doing, cutie?" he mumbles. His breath smells like whiskey and beef jerky. I hurry past him as he stumbles toward a dimly lit bar.

Brooklyn lives on the first floor of a cheap apartment complex. It's set up to look like a motel. All the apartment doors face an open-air hallway protected only by the cheap, painted aluminum guardrail. Just beyond the edge of the property, I can see the service road that leads to the tattoo parlor.

A sound like a gunshot echoes down the dark alley near her street. I freeze, every muscle in my body tensing to run. Then a car engine sputters on, and an old Buick pulls away from the curb. Not a gunshot—a car backfiring. I exhale and keep moving. The sooner I make it to Brooklyn's place, the better.

Even if she hadn't slipped me the address in English lit class, I wouldn't have trouble finding Brooklyn's party. The music's so loud it vibrates through the parking lot, and the apartment door hangs open. Girls in short skirts and pierced, tattooed guys lounge against the wall, drinking from red Solo cups and smoking cigarettes that smell like pine needles. Green paint bubbles up around where they stubbed the butts out on the walls. Either they're all over twenty-one, or this isn't the kind of neighborhood that calls the cops for underage drinking.

"Hey, little girl!" someone calls, startling me. I turn just as a large bald guy approaches. He towers above me, and he has to weigh at least two hundred pounds. He wears all black, and a white-and-black skull tattoo covers his face and bald head. It looks like he doesn't have any skin.

I start to turn back around, hoping he's not talking to me. He grabs my arm.

"Don't be like that. I'm talking to you," he says. Deep black lines shadow his eyes, and tattoos of teeth stretch down over his lips. "I've got a question."

"Shoot," I say, struggling to keep my voice steady. The man's lips part, but I can't tell if he's smiling at me or grimacing.

"My friends and I are taking a poll." He nods to a group of people standing by the apartment door. They're all pierced and tattooed, but next to Skull Guy they look like members of a church group. "If you could choose how you were going to die, would you rather be beaten to death with a shovel or have your face eaten off?"

I swallow, trying to keep my nerves from showing on my face. The guy might be freaky looking, but he just wants to get a reaction out of me. It's all just part of his game.

"I'd go for the face," I say, meeting his gaze. "I'd want to look my killer in the eye."

This time I'm sure Skull Guy smiles at me. The white-and-black cheekbone tattoos stretch across his face when his lips part. "Solid," he says, bumping my fist.

I nod at a couple more people as I walk past, trying to look like I belong. The music pounds around me, an insistent *bomp bomp bomp*. Once inside, I push my sweat-shirt hood back and glance around the room. It's smoky and dark. Bodies crowd around me, packed so tightly I can't move without bumping someone's arm or back. The floor is sticky, littered with empty beer cans.

I can't believe I worried this would be anything like my last party. It's a completely different world. I've never heard the music before, and I don't think any of the people here actually go to our school. A girl with long, white-blond hair and glassy eyes passes a tiny bag of powder to another girl in a leather jacket, then walks away without glancing at her. I weave through the crowd to a table covered in booze and beer. I grab the single can of off-brand soda sitting next to a case of PBR, just so I have something to do with my hands.

A voice rises above the music, startling me. "Sofia!"

I turn and, through the sea of people pushing in on me, spot Charlie waving his hands above his head like he's signaling planes. If I were a cartoon character, my mouth would drop to the floor and exclamation points would shoot out of my eyes—that's how excited I am to see him standing there, wearing a worn T-shirt with some faded sports logo on it and a dark gray zip-up sweatshirt. He moves around a crowd of guys to stand in front of me and says something I can't hear over the noise. I smile so wide the corners of my mouth threaten to split.

"What?" I shout.

He grins back at me, and even in the dark I notice the dimple in his cheek. Pushing the hair from my neck, he leans in close enough that his breath warms my skin.

"It's loud," he says. "Wanna go outside?"

"Sure."

Charlie takes my hand, and we head for the back of the apartment to a smudged sliding glass door. I crack open my soda as Charlie pushes through the door and we slip outside. Cold air rushes to greet me, and I shiver, almost glad the can is warm, even if the soda tastes terrible.

"You seem to be the only other person here not trying to get completely hammered," Charlie says once we've left the pounding music behind.

"I'm not a big drinker," I say. Charlie nods.

"Me neither." He smiles at me again, that dimple appearing in his cheek. My stomach flips.

"I'm glad you're here. I don't really know anyone else." Charlie glances around at the kids sprawled on lawn chairs and hovering near the apartment door. At first I don't recognize any of them, either, but then I spot Tom wearing a backward baseball cap. He leans forward, passing his cigarette to a cute girl with black dreadlocks and thick glasses. The girl giggles at something he says, then leans in to kiss him. I cringe. Grace would be devastated.

Charlie sees him, too. "I know Tom, I guess. But he's been preoccupied. Josh said he was coming, but I haven't seen him. And now I know you."

"Josh is coming to this party?" I didn't think this was Josh's scene—he seems so preppy, like Riley. Charlie shrugs.

I glance around at the patchy grass and dirty white lawn chairs. Beyond them, I see the outlines of a slide, a swing set, and what I assume is a pool surrounded by high wooden fencing. Despite the cold weather, I hear giggling and splashing.

A smile creeps across my face. I pull on Charlie's sleeve. "Come on. I have a plan."

"Are we going swimming?" Charlie asks when I start to lead him toward the pool.

"It's, like, fifty degrees out!" I pull my sweatshirt tighter around my shoulders. "Besides, I don't have a suit."

"Why should that stop you?"

I groan and push him toward the slide instead. The playground equipment is made of that old steel that isn't used at schools anymore, because people are afraid kids will impale themselves on the sharp metal while playing. I approach the slide hesitantly and test the bottom ladder rung to make sure it'll hold my weight.

"Are you serious?" Charlie says. I raise an eyebrow in challenge.

"It's either the slide with me, or you go back to the party to hang out with people who don't even remember their names. Your choice."

Charlie purses his lips, pretending to think this over. "Which people, exactly?"

I pick up a rock and threaten to throw it at him, and he raises his hands in surrender, laughing. "Kidding, kidding." He jogs to the bottom of the slide and crouches down. "Okay, go. I'll catch you."

"I don't need you to catch me," I say. I set my soda down on the ground and climb up the ladder, perching on top of the slide. Charlie grins.

"Of course you do." He grabs the sides of the slide with both hands and shakes, causing the entire thing to rattle. "This thing is a death trap."

Despite the coolness of the night, the metal is warm beneath my hands. I push myself down, and as I start to gather speed, I shriek. Charlie grabs my shoulders before I hit the dirt and holds me steady.

"You okay?" he asks. He actually looks concerned. "I can't believe they let kids on that thing."

"Your turn," I say, pushing myself back to my feet.

Charlie grins and races around to the ladder. The entire slide rocks as he climbs, the metal creaking so badly I'm convinced it's about to fall apart.

"Shit," Charlie says as he settles at the top. "Now I have so much more respect for you for going first."

"Well, I'm a rebel."

"Here goes nothing." Charlie pushes off and shoots down the slide. Somewhere along the way he goes into warp speed, and then he's not sliding anymore—he's flying—and I can't move out of the way before he tumbles into me. We both roll backward, hitting the dirt in a tangle of limbs.

"I'm so sorry," he says, pushing himself onto an elbow. He doesn't roll off me right away. "Did I break you?"

"No." I keep my arms still because I don't trust myself not to grab his sweatshirt and pull him even closer. I clear my throat. "You're . . . fine."

Charlie tilts his head, and I wonder if he can tell what I'm thinking. "I'm really glad you're here, Sofia," he says.

"Yeah, well, I did break your fall," I say. He still doesn't move away from me. He brushes a curl off my forehead and shakes his head like I'm missing something.

"It's not just that. I'm glad to see *you*."

The night instantly grows ten degrees warmer. "Why?"

"You're joking, right?" Charlie eyes lose focus. He's about to kiss me. I inhale, hoping the warm soda hasn't made my mouth taste gross. But he just runs his thumb along my jaw, tracing from my ear to my chin, like he's memorizing my face.

"I like you, okay? You're different from girls around here." He leans toward me again, his eyes closing. This time he hesitates an inch away from me.

"Is this okay?" he asks.

"Yeah." I've barely spoken when he presses his mouth to mine—tentative first, then harder, hungrier. He parts my lips with his tongue and slides his fingers into my hair, pulling me closer, until there's not an inch of his body that isn't pressed against mine. I stop thinking and just react, letting my hips and chest rise and fall with his. One hand is tangled in my hair and another tugging at the waistband of my jeans. He slips his fingers through my curls as he moves his hand down to trace the skin from my neck to my collarbone, sending shivers through my entire body. Decades pass before Charlie pulls away. His hair sticks out from his head in all angles, and I itch to reach for it again, to smooth it back behind his ears. All the blood in his head seems to have rushed to his lips, because they're bright red and swollen from kissing me.

His nose brushes against mine. "You taste minty," he says into my mouth, leaning in to kiss me again.

The giggling in the swimming pool rises in a shriek of laughter and then cuts off abruptly. Charlie hesitates and reluctantly pulls his lips away from mine.

"What do you think they're doing?" I ask. "Should we find out?"

Charlie pushes himself to his feet, then leans over to give me his hand. "Only if it'll help convince you that swimsuits are optional."

"Unlikely," I say, but I follow him toward the pool anyway. There are gaps in the fence, each about one inch wide. I squint into the gaps, but I can't make out entire people—just jumbled shapes. Charlie comes up behind me. Circling my waist with his arms, he starts to kiss my neck.

"I thought we were spying," I whisper.

"Spies do this."

Just beyond the fence a girl says something, but the wind snatches away her words. I lean in closer, pressing my eye against the largest gap.

Brooklyn stands at the top of the plastic staircase leading into a hot tub, holding the stub of a cigarette between two fingers. Black swimsuit bottoms hang low on her hips, and she has a white tank top knotted above her waist. The tank top is wet and pasted to her skin in patches, making it easy to see she's not wearing a bra.

"What are they doing?" Charlie whispers. I shush

him, lifting a finger to my mouth. There's a boy in the hot tub, too, his brown hair slicked up in wet spikes. Thin lines of steam rise from the tub, mingling with the smoke from Brooklyn's cigarette.

"Ever done it in a hot tub?" Brooklyn asks, her mouth curling. She's wearing dark red lipstick that smudges across her cigarette. The boy stands, water dripping from his faded navy boxers. He grabs Brooklyn and spins her around.

I immediately recognize the light brown eyes, the cleft chin. Josh. *Riley's* Josh.

I press my face closer to the fence. Josh sets Brooklyn back down and pulls her to his chest. She drops her cigarette into the water behind her, then lifts her face up to his. They kiss long and deep, and I blush even harder.

Brooklyn looks up, and her eyes find the exact spot in the fence where I'm watching. It's like someone has touched an icy finger to the lowest part of my back and runs it up the length of my spine. She wraps her arms around Josh's neck and kisses him again, possessively, her red-painted mouth mashing against his teeth as she pulls him closer. The whole time, she never takes her eyes away from the fence. From me.

It's like a dare. A challenge. I pull away from the fence and turn back to Charlie, feeling as though I've had the wind knocked out of me.

"Sofia, what's wrong?" Charlie asks. I shake my head. "I've got to go," I say.

* * *

I make my way to Riley's house, following a long, curved road that dead-ends onto Riley's street. Gnarly trees line the sidewalks. The houses sit back far from the street, their windows dark. Overhanging branches send skeletal shadows over their yards.

A bird squawks above me, rustling the tree branches as it flies away.

"Crap," I mutter, trying to still my rapidly beating heart. I ran most of the way here, not because I wanted to get to Riley, but because I didn't want to spend any more time in Brooklyn's neighborhood. In fact, now that I'm here I wish the trip had taken longer.

I pass a few more towering houses before I locate Riley's. Her house is a mini-mansion. A wide white porch wraps around front, and Greek-style pillars stand on either side of the double doors. I ring the bell, and a tinny *ding-dong* echoes inside.

A tiny green garden snake slivers across the wooden porch, its body undulating over the concrete. I cringe and cross my arms over my chest. A second later it disappears behind a heavy clay flowerpot.

Footsteps sound just inside the house, then the door swings open.

"Sofia?" Riley leans a cheek against the edge of the door, considering me. "Are you okay?"

"I'm sorry, I tried to call." I try to catch my breath. "Can I come in?"

The corner of Riley's mouth twitches upward, and her face grows several degrees warmer. "Of course. You want something to drink?"

"Um, sure."

Riley steps back, opening the door into a foyer with high ceilings and real marble floors. I step inside, momentarily distracted. Beautifully posed photographs of Riley sandwiched between her parents cover the walls, all three wearing matching preppy-chic. I gape at them, amazed at how perfect everyone looks, like they're posing for a catalog.

"Your parents look nice." I stop in front of one of the photographs. Riley's family is dressed entirely in white and they're sitting on a bench in front their lake house. Despite what I saw at Brooklyn's party, I find myself wishing I could step into Riley's life for a day or two, just to see what it's like. It must be nice to have the perfect family, the perfect house, the perfect friends.

Riley stops next to me, staring at the photographs without blinking. "Come on," she says.

"The kitchen's this way."

I follow her down a white-carpeted hallway and

into a huge kitchen with stainless steel appliances and cabinets made of deep, dark wood. Gray tile covers the floors, and the only light comes from the window over the sink, where moonlight filters in through gauzy curtains. Riley motions for me to sit on one of the bar stools at an island in the middle of the room.

"Is something wrong?" She opens the fridge and pulls out a pitcher of water. I see just enough of the inside of her fridge to notice most of the shelves are bare. I clear my throat. I spent the entire walk trying to come up with something to say, but every time words formed in my head I was hit by a sudden, overwhelming feeling of guilt—like I'd been the one making out with Josh instead of Brooklyn.

Riley puts the pitcher on the counter, considering me. In the dim light her blue eyes look gray.

"Sweetie, what is it?" Her forehead wrinkles in confusion. I look down at my sneakers, unable to meet her eyes. If I'd found Brooklyn as soon as I got to the party instead of rolling around on the ground with Charlie, none of this would have happened.

"I . . ." I shift on my bar stool. Footsteps sound in the other room, cutting me off. Riley's head jerks up as a woman wearing a silky white robe comes into the kitchen. Her glass is empty except for a few ice cubes.

"Hi, girls," she says with a weak smile. She must be

Riley's mother—Mrs. Howard—but she looks nothing like the person from the photographs in the hall. Her hair falls above her shoulders; it looks like a trendy cut that's grown out. Her face is strange, too—there's something about her features that don't match up with where I expect them to be. Her cheeks have a hollow look, like they're going to cave in.

She crosses the kitchen, the ice in her glass clinking. She pulls a bottle of something clear out of the freezer, and when she bends over, her robe gapes open and I have to avert my eyes to keep from seeing her bare chest.

"You girls having fun?" Mrs. Howard asks.

"A blast," Riley deadpans. "Come on, Sofia. We'll have more privacy in my room."

"Nice to meet you," I mutter, then follow Riley upstairs, wondering if her father is behind one of the heavy doors lining the hallway. The thickly carpeted floor quiets our footsteps.

Riley pushes open a door at the end of the hallway, revealing a bedroom larger than the master suite at my house. Old-fashioned floral wallpaper covers the walls, and heavy velvet curtains hang over the windows. It's so dark I have to squint to see the edges of the furniture. An ornate wooden cross hangs above her door.

"Make yourself at home." Riley crosses the room to turn on a light and settles herself in the faded pink armchair in front of a vintage vanity table. Glass bottles of makeup cover the table, along with half-burned candles and lacy fabric that looks like a scarf. Alexis's and Grace's pictures crowd the mirror, leaving only a tiny circle in the center uncovered. I stop in front of the vanity, smoothing a dog-eared snapshot. If I weren't here for such an awful reason, I'd make Riley tell me the story behind every photograph. I'd take pictures of the two of us on my phone, hoping I'd make it to the mirror, too.

To the left of the mirror stands an old porcelain doll with a cracked face and brown curls like Riley's. The doll's cloudy glass eyes follow me as I perch on the edge of Riley's bed.

I open my mouth and try to speak, but I can't say the words out loud. *Your boyfriend is cheating on you.*

"Sof?" Riley leans forward, putting a hand on my knee. "What is it?" Something passes over her eyes, and she leans away, her back ruler-straight. She speaks in a whisper, "Did something happen at the party?"

I take a deep breath. "Riley, you have to break up with Josh," I blurt out.

A crease forms between Riley's eyes. "What?"

"I *saw* him," I say, quickly so I don't lose my nerve. "With Brooklyn just now."

Understanding passes over Riley's face, and the

crease disappears from between her eyes. She opens her mouth, then closes it again.

"You saw them together," she says, her voice steady. She squeezes her eyes shut, and I expect her to start crying, but her eyes are dry when she blinks them open again. "Were they having sex?"

"No. Just kissing." Brooklyn's words echo in my head as soon as I say this. *Ever done it in a hot tub?*

Riley nods. She pushes herself out of her chair and starts pacing the length of her room. She stops in front of the door and presses a hand against the wood, closing her eyes. I push myself to my feet to give her a hug when her lips start to move silently. She's not crying—she's praying.

"Amen," she whispers, and her eyes flicker open. She stares at her door without saying a word.

"Riley, I'm so sorry." My shoulders tighten, and I stand a little straighter. "I came right here after I saw them. I just thought you should know."

"Sof, it's okay," Riley says. "I prayed, and I think it's obvious what we need to do. Brooklyn is lost. We have to help her."

"You want to *help* Brooklyn?" I gape at Riley, confused. "But what about Josh? Aren't you pissed?"

"Josh strayed from God," Riley says. "Yeah, it hurts, but I believe he'll find his way back to the Lord. But

Brooklyn . . . don't you get it, Sofia? This just *proves* she needs our help. Brooklyn has to be fixed."

A smile flutters across Riley's face. It reminds me of when I first met her, when her smile never seemed to spread past her lips, leaving her eyes cold and empty. Now, though, her eyes are bright with a kind of manic energy. When she talks again, her words tumble into one another, like they're racing to get out of her mouth.

"We thought Brooklyn was rebelling, but this is worse. Some people have evil inside them, Sofia. Brooklyn needs us."

The word *evil* still seems too strong to me, but I can't argue with Riley after what I saw. If this is what she needs to get over Josh, I can be there for her. I squeeze her arm. "How do we do that?"

"Don't worry." Riley places her hand over mine and squeezes back. "You don't have to do anything. I have a plan."

# CHAPTER SEVEN

A floorboard creaks somewhere in the house, jerking me from sleep. I force my eyes open, not sure if what I heard was real or an echo from a dream.

A heavy footstep thuds against the floor downstairs. Then silence.

I sit up, my comforter falling to my lap. My heart pounds in my ears. It could be Mom going downstairs for a glass of water. But that's unlikely. Most nights she takes insanely strong sleeping pills and is out like the dead till morning.

I push back the rest of my blankets and slip from the bed. The floor freezes my bare feet, and I shiver as I stumble for the door. There's no moon tonight, leaving my room so dark I can't see my arms stretched in front of me.

The house falls silent. I'm being silly. Even if it wasn't Mom, that sound could have been a million things: the house settling or wind pounding at the windows. Still, I hold my breath until I find the door with my fingers. I press my ear to the wood, listening for a sound in the hallway.

The top stair groans: another footstep. Someone's out there.

I stumble backward and crash into my desk. There's another creak, this one outside my door.

"Who's there?" I whisper. I step away from my desk, forcing myself toward the door. Louder, I ask, "Mom? Is that you?"

It's too dark to see, but I hear my door latch click and feel the air move as the door swings open. A fingernails-on-sandpaper scratch cuts through the silence, and I smell sulfur. Blue-orange light flickers to life.

I blink against the sudden brightness, and, as my eyes focus, I make out a lit match and a face. Light dances in Riley's eyes. She puts a finger to her lips. *Quiet.*

"You scared me to death!" I take a deep breath to get rid of the last of my fear and lean against my desk, my heart still thudding like crazy. "How did you get in?"

She doesn't answer, but her eyebrow twitches higher. Her eyes are manic, wide and dark, her pupils dilated in twin black pools. An emotion I can't place flickers across her face, and my question changes from *how* she got in to *why*.

"Hurry," she whispers. The match burns down to her fingertips, and she shakes it out. A silver curl of smoke stretches to the ceiling. "I want to show you something."

This has to be about Josh. I bet the others are waiting at the house for us, and we'll spend the night eating ice cream and complaining to one another about what jerks guys are. My fear flips into relief.

I grab my sneakers, then push my bedroom door open. Riley follows silently. Once in the hallway I hesitate, glancing at my mom's door. I motion for Riley to keep quiet as we start down the stairs.

We hurry out of my house, stopping for Riley to grab a pair of gray sneakers she'd hidden behind the potted plant on our front porch. She slides them onto her bare feet without untying them first, and we head down the street.

The wind slices through the sleeves of my sweater and coaxes goose bumps from my skin. I press my lips together to keep my teeth from chattering and pull my sweater over my hands. Despite Riley's bare legs, she doesn't shiver.

I notice a shadow crouched on the porch steps as we near the abandoned house: Grace. She looks plainer than I've ever seen her, in a black T-shirt, jeans, and faded sneakers. The hood of her giraffe-print sweatshirt hides her hair.

"Hey, Grace," I say as I pass her on the steps.

"Hey," she echoes hollowly. Her eyes don't quite focus, and she doesn't acknowledge Riley at all. You'd think she was the one whose boyfriend just cheated on her.

"Is she okay?" I ask. Riley pushes the front door open, and the two of us slip inside.

"Grace? Probably just tired. Come on—it's this way."

I ease the door shut behind me and realize a doorknob has been added where there wasn't one before. Riley notices my confusion and pulls a key out of the pocket of her jeans. "Can never be too careful," she says, as if that answers everything.

We walk past the living room, where the sleeping bags are rolled and stacked next to the pillows in a corner. None of the tea lights are lit, and it makes this place feel emptier than before. I realize how alone we are out here, with nothing but dirt and the skeletons of half-built houses surrounding us. Wind rattles the plastic at the windows. I imagine it rolling over miles of empty land to press against this house, and suddenly it seems strong enough to rip off walls.

"We're going to the basement," Riley says, opening a door I thought was a closet. I peer down the stairs, but I can't see past the concrete wall below. The rest of the basement is dark.

"What's down there?"

"A surprise," Riley says. The first step creaks beneath her bare foot. She takes me by the arm. "Don't be scared."

I start down the stairs with her, focused on placing one foot in front of the other. Cold air creeps in through the concrete walls and floor, holding a damp scent of dust and something I can't place. I wrinkle my nose as we make our way down. It smells metallic, like pennies.

There's a muffled whimper deep in the basement, like someone crying into a pillow. I freeze on the bottom step.

"Riley . . ." I still can't see past the concrete wall, and I suddenly want to keep it that way. But Riley tugs on my arm, her fingernails pricking the skin on my wrist. My feet move forward on their own.

"It's okay, Sof," she says, and I let her lead me around the corner.

The blue oil lamp from upstairs sits on a table near the far wall, casting a wedge of flickering light over the concrete. Alexis crouches over the lamp, messing with a lever on the side. There's a flicker of movement, like an arm reaching out of the shadows behind her. I jerk my head around to stare, praying it was just a trick of the light.

The lamp's tiny flame dances higher, illuminating Brooklyn's crumpled body. Duct tape winds around her mouth and cheeks, plastering her short, sweaty hair to her head. She's tied to a wooden pillar in the middle of the room, her arms pressed against her sides, and her legs trapped beneath her.

Fear rises in my chest, but I push it back down. This is a joke. They must've set it up to mess with me. I laugh nervously, but then Brooklyn raises her head and shakes the matted hair from her eyes. Her gaze shifts to mine, and it's like I've been plunged in cold water. The fear in Brooklyn's eyes is real.

"Riley." My voice is hoarse, a whisper. "What did you do?"

"What did I *do*?" Riley's voice hits the concrete like a slap. Brooklyn jerks at the sound, but her red eyes stay fixed on me. "We talked about this, Sofia." Riley crosses the room to Alexis and picks up a black backpack. She reaches inside and pulls out a butcher knife. Brooklyn breathes in through her nose with a shaky sob, and I throw a hand over my mouth.

"Shit! Riley, why do you have that?"

"I'm going to get the evil out of her." Riley turns the knife to catch the glare of the lamp. I glance back at Brooklyn. The ropes rubbed the skin around her wrists raw, and her hair's drenched with sweat, but otherwise she's unhurt. She mostly just looks scared. I exhale. There's still time to fix this.

"Riley, give me the knife," I say, holding out my hand. The blade distorts my reflection, making my forehead too long, my eyes beady pricks of black. I look like a monster.

"Don't be silly, Sofia." Riley pulls the knife to her side and wraps her fingers around it possessively. "We talked about this. You said we're in this together."

Riley's delusional. We talked about helping her, not *kidnapping* her. Brooklyn hasn't taken her eyes off the knife. Her face twists in fear, crinkling the edges of the duct tape. I start to cross the basement, but Alexis steps in front of me, blocking my way.

"Let me through," I demand. Alexis crosses her arms over her chest and glances at Riley over my shoulder. Brooklyn shifts on the concrete behind her. The ropes binding her wrists tighten with a groan as she moves. "Alexis, we have to untie her!"

"This is for her own good, Sofia." Riley steps up behind me and places a hand on my shoulder to prevent me from moving any closer to Brooklyn. A chill spreads from the tips of my fingers to the small of my back. "Alexis, did you pack everything?" Riley shifts the backpack in her arms, grimacing under its weight.

"I think so." Alexis watches Riley from beneath the

veil of her own pale white-blond hair. I can't tell if she's as freaked out as I am, but it's obvious she's not going to do anything to stop this.

"What's in there?" I ask, eyeing the backpack.

"Very important supplies." Riley unzips the bag and removes jars of water and salt, three bottles of wine, and a heavy, leather-bound Bible. She sets the items on the floor and reaches into the bag again. I expect more knives, but Riley pulls out a wooden cross.

Suddenly something clicks. "This is an exorcism."

"Lexie taught me how to perform one," Riley says. She sets the knife down on the floor and picks up the bottle of wine, yanking out the cork.

"We're going to draw the demon out of Brooklyn," Alexis explains. "Most priests use holy water or a cross, sometimes blessed salt."

I decide to skip over the "demon" comment and move to the most obvious flaw in their plan. "But none of us is a priest."

"We don't need to be," Alexis says. "That's what I was telling Riley. Anyone can perform an exorcism as long as they're filled with the Holy Spirit. And the more true believers you have with you the stronger you are. With you and Grace, we have four."

"Don't be scared, Sof," Riley says, taking a drink of wine. "This'll be fun."

I nod woodenly. None of their supplies are too terrible, aside from the knife. Maybe they'll just throw some water at Brooklyn and chant for a while. They probably only brought the knife to freak her out—punishment for screwing around with Josh. I breathe in deeply, trying to calm my nerves. This could still be okay.

But then I glance up, meeting Brooklyn's red-rimmed eyes. Her shoulders rise and fall in silent sobs and sweat, and tears mingle with her eyeliner, sending thick black lines streaming down her face. This isn't a prank. Riley didn't say she wanted to punish Brooklyn—she said she wanted to *save* her, and for some reason that involves a knife and holding a girl prisoner in the basement.

"I can't do this," I say. I ease my foot off the floor and move it behind me, slowly backing toward the staircase. My legs are so numb I worry I might collapse. "I have to go."

I turn and stumble toward the staircase without waiting for Riley to answer. When I reach the concrete wall, I break into a run, my shoes slipping against the steps. My brain is moving too quickly, telling me I'm overreacting, that nothing's wrong. At the same time my palms start to sweat and my knees shake. My body wants to get as far away from here as possible.

Once I'm through the basement door, time speeds up. My heart pounds in my ears, making it impossible to think. I tear through the kitchen, moving so quickly I smack an arm against the doorframe and stumble into the hall, landing *hard* on my knees. Pain shoots up my legs. But I grit my teeth and push myself to my feet and run.

The shadows in the living room seem to reach for me as I race past. I glance outside when I get to the front door, but Grace isn't on the porch anymore. I don't stop to think about where she might've gone. My hands tremble so badly the doorknob rattles as I work the lock, but, finally, my fingers manage to twist the deadbolt. I turn the knob and pull.

The door doesn't budge. I pull harder. The knob turns easily, but the door itself stays firmly shut. Finally, I glance up. There's a lock screwed into the doorframe, held shut with a heavy, metal padlock.

*"Shit."* My voice is barely a whisper, but it seems to boom around me. I think of what Riley said when I saw the new doorknob. *Can never be too careful.*

I stumble back down the hall, pulling open the first door I see. It's a bedroom, with two windows on the far wall. I race across the room and feel for the edge of the window with my fingers. My hand brushes against metal. My heart sinks.

Nails line the window frame, sealing it shut. Some are driven deep into the wood, and some are long and crooked, jutting awkwardly out of the frame. A single bent nail lies on the sill, next to a wobbly sketch of a heart that someone etched into the wood.

For a long moment I just stare at the nails, trying to keep myself from hyperventilating or dissolving into tears. Riley isn't crazy enough to lock us all in here, to nail the windows shut so we can't leave. But even as this thought occurs to me, I know it's exactly what she's done. I'm trapped here with her—we all are.

My legs shake as I move backward. I start opening doors at random, desperately searching for an exit Riley might have missed. My breathing gets more ragged as I run from one empty room to another. I claw at the nails in the windowsills until my fingers bleed, but they don't budge. Riley must've used a nail gun.

Finally I stumble into a bathroom. There's only one window here, the kind you crank with a lever to open. There aren't nails sticking out of the frame. I release a shaky, desperate sob.

I grip the lever with both hands. The plastic notch digs into my skin as I yank it around and around. The window jerks and starts, opening at an angle and letting cold air seep into the bathroom. Clouds hide the moon, leaving the night perfectly dark. Cicadas buzz in the grass.

I stop cranking once there's a gap wide enough for me to climb through. The cicadas sound louder, but maybe that's just because my heartbeat has slowed. I'm going to make it. I'm going to get out of here, and I'm going to call the cops. Wiping my sweaty hands on my jeans, I lean forward, knuckles white as I wrap my fingers around the sill.

A hand slaps the outside of the glass, slamming the window shut on my fingers.

Bright, hot pain rips through my hands. I cry out and try to pull away, but the window pins my fingers in place. The clouds move, bathing Riley in moonlight.

She studies me with those gray eyes, then leans into the window with her shoulder, pressing it against my fingers.

"Can't let you leave now, Sof." Riley moves away from the glass, and the window swings open. I snatch my hands away, my breathing ragged. Blood oozes around my knuckles and drips down my wrist, staining the sleeves of my cardigan.

"Clean yourself up," Riley says. "We're just getting started."

# CHAPTER EIGHT

I drop to my knees on the cold bathroom floor and fumble for the roll of toilet paper next to the toilet, clumsily mopping up the blood dripping from my fingers. I open my hand, then close it again, testing. Nothing's broken.

Someone pounds at the door. "Hurry up, Sof." The wood muffles Riley's voice. "We're waiting."

I take two deep breaths. My lungs burn and my head feels dizzy. It's just Riley. Riley, who gossiped with me about boys while drinking red wine. Riley, who insisted I eat with her after finding that dead cat. She's not crazy—she just snapped. The real Riley's still in there.

Besides, I can't stay in the bathroom forever. I lick my thumb and wipe the blood from my knuckles. Then I push the door open.

The moonlight from the bathroom window illuminates Riley's narrow shoulders and long, skinny arms. She cocks her head, and her dark curls pool on one shoulder. She looks just like a doll.

"Go back to the basement," she says. "I need to take care of that."

She nods at the bathroom. She's holding a nail gun. She pushes past me to nail the last remaining exit in this house shut.

"Riley, think about this," I say. Riley turns. She doesn't smile, but the creases around her eyes and mouth soften. She takes my hand, squeezing just above my wrist.

"I know you're scared, Sofia," she says. "I know that's why you tried to run. But if you're not with me, you're against me."

She tightens her grip, just enough to pinch the skin at my wrist. I cringe and pull my arm away.

"I'm with you," I say, glancing down at the nail gun.

"Good," Riley says. "Now go."

Shadows stretch across the hallway, making it hard to see where I'm going. I find a light switch in the kitchen and flip it on and then off, but nothing happens. Cursing, I push the basement door open, gripping for the banister in the dark. I feel for the top step with the toe of my sneaker.

Grace peeks around the concrete wall, hovering at the bottom of the stairs. "Are you coming down?"

"Grace," I say, relieved. Shadows hide her face, so I picture the hollow, unfocused expression she wore on the porch. Alexis will side with Riley no matter what, but Grace is different. She can't think what's going on down there is okay. "I think Riley . . ."

The basement door opens behind me, cutting me off. I turn.

Riley steps onto the staircase. Only the outline of her narrow body is visible in the dim light. She pulls the door shut, and something metallic thumps against the wood. I shift my eyes to the door, noticing a thick padlock attached to the frame.

"What is that?"

"Riley put it up," Grace says.

"We don't want anyone sneaking in on us," Riley adds.

I blink against the darkness. She clicks the lock closed, then slips the key into her pocket. She's not locking everyone else out; she's locking us in.

"Hurry up, girls," Riley says, starting down the stairs. "We have work to do."

Grace shuffles farther into the basement without

a word. I follow, but every time I place my foot on a creaky step a new image flashes through my head: first the backpack filled with wine and holy water, then the windows nailed shut, and now the brand-new padlock attached to the door. It must've taken days to do all this, weeks maybe. I picture Riley nailing the upstairs window shut seconds before we all arrived at the house to drink wine and gossip about Josh, Riley stopping at the hardware store to buy a new padlock on the afternoon I walked to the tattoo parlor with Brooklyn. I wipe my sweaty palms on my jeans.

Alexis is crouched next to Brooklyn, whispering. She glances up as the three of us approach and pushes her wispy hair behind one ear. She's surrounded Brooklyn with flickering candles. She motions to the one she's still holding.

"I read that demons are afraid of fire," she says, blinking her wide eyes.

"Good plan, Lexie," Riley coos. "It's like we're surrounding her with a circle of light, to pull her away from the darkness."

Riley squeezes my shoulder. "Yeah, good thinking," I add, and she beams at me.

Alexis puts the last candle down on the floor and stands. "We're all here now. We should get started."

She reaches for my hand while Riley takes the other

one. Together with Grace we form a semicircle around Brooklyn. I don't want to look at her, but I don't have a choice, so I lift my eyes.

A sweaty strand of white-blond hair hangs over Brooklyn's face, fluttering around her nose every time she exhales. Thick black eyeliner runs down her cheeks like tears. I tighten my grip on Riley's hand. We just have to get through the exorcism. This could still be okay.

"We have to be right with God before we can begin," Alexis explains. Brooklyn shifts her combat boot–covered foot. The sole screeches over the concrete floor. "If we want him to drive the demon away, we have to confess our own sins and ask for his forgiveness."

An uneasy silence stretches between us, broken only by the flames licking the candlewicks. I'm not sure I want to know their sins.

"I guess I'll go first," Grace says, fumbling with her sweatshirt zipper. She stares at her sneakers while she speaks, like she's telling her story to them instead of us. "I need a scholarship in order to afford a good college, so I have to get perfect grades. Calculus has been kicking my butt, though, and last week I stole some of my little brother's Ritalin. He has ADD, and the pills are supposed to help him concentrate. I figured they'd be good for studying."

"Oh, Grace," Riley says. "Why didn't you tell us you were struggling?"

"I was embarrassed," she says, dropping her hand from her zipper. "It was just once. They helped get me through the test, but I felt woozy the whole time. I'm never taking them again."

Riley matches Grace's gaze as she lifts her head. "Good."

Wind presses against the tiny, rectangular window near the basement ceiling, making the glass groan. Yesterday Grace's confession might have shocked me, but in light of everything else, pill popping is pretty tame.

"Your turn," Riley says, nodding at Alexis.

Alexis drops Grace's hand and weaves a strand of her long, blond hair around a finger. She turns to me as she begins, "Riley and Grace already know this, but my older sister, Carly, has been in the hospital for the past several months. What should be her best year as a senior she's spending in a coma, all because she accidentally ate one little peanut." Alexis's accent deepens as she speaks, and she pauses in all the right places, as if she's told this story many times before. She whispers the word *coma* like it's too painful to say out loud.

Riley clears her throat. "That isn't your fault, Lexie," she says.

Alexis winds the blond curl tighter and tighter around her finger. "It's not that. I should be sad all the time, but I'm just . . . not." The candlelight flickers, reflecting in Alexis's wide, dark eyes. "Things have been easier with her gone," she continues. "I don't have to compete with her, and we don't fight anymore. There are days I wish she'd never wake up."

"But she's your sister," Grace says.

"I know," Alexis says. I can tell Alexis feels tortured by the way her voice has started to shake. But still, there's something that feels off about her confession. "I pray for forgiveness every day. God knows I want Carly to be okay."

Grace nods, but her mouth twists in disgust. What kind of person wishes her own sister would stay in a coma?

"We forgive you, Lexie," Riley assures her. "Carly will wake up before you know it, and you'll be happy to have her back. I'm sure of it."

The wind rises to a howl. Grace gives Alexis an uneasy smile, and Alexis exhales in relief.

"I'll go next," Riley says. She squares her shoulders and deliberately softens her eyes. "I always told you Josh and I were waiting for marriage, but, well, this summer at the lake house things got a little out of control."

"Seriously?" Grace's eyes widen. "Why didn't you tell us?"

"Yeah, how out of control?" Alexis adds.

"We didn't go all the way, but we got close. I stopped

him before we went too far. But sometimes, I wonder what would have happened if I didn't. It's probably my fault that . . ." Her voice cracks and she shakes her head, unable to finish her sentence. She lifts the bottle of wine to her lips, closing her eyes as she takes a drink. Lowering it, she whispers, "Forgive me, Lord."

Another silence stretches between us, this one charged. Alexis squeezes my hand so tightly my fingers go numb, and Grace glares at her sneakers, refusing to meet anyone's eyes. Riley nudges me. "Sof? Your turn now. You can tell us anything."

I stare at the floor as their eyes settle on me. I'd been so distracted by their stories I almost forgot I had to share my own. My skin prickles, and the memory unfolds in my head before I can say a word.

*I slide onto my bar stool in biology class and slip a Q-tip into a sandwich bag, writing the label with a Sharpie. I'm hunched over the table when something pokes me in the head.*

*"Hey!" I say, turning around. Erin stands behind me, a Q-tip in her hand. She's wearing a leather tank top with a V-neck so low it's impossible for her to wear a bra.*

*"Lila and I have a bet going on what the germiest thing in the classroom's going to be," Erin says, dropping the Q-tip into a sandwich bag. "My money's on your greasy-ass hair."*

*She doesn't laugh, but the students behind her giggle and*

*snicker into their hands. I glance at Karen, who's standing across the room with Lila. She doesn't look as amused as everyone else, but she stares at her shoes and doesn't say a word.*

*Tears prick the corners of my eyes, but I know the worst thing I can do is cry. Instead I push back my stool and walk, quickly, from the room. By the time I get to the hallway my shoulders shake, and it's all I can do to hold back the sobs. I hear them laughing behind me. The sound echoes in my head.*

"Sof?" Riley's voice brings me back to the present, and my eyes flicker open.

Alexis touches my arm. "It's okay, we're here for you."

I swallow, shaking the memory away. Almost without realizing it, I start picking at the skin around my cuticles.

"I didn't fit in at my last school. There were these girls in my science class who always made fun of me. And . . ." I bite off the end of my sentence, not sure how to finish. Riley nudges me with her shoulder.

"And what?"

I pull at the skin around my thumbnail. "I got into a fight with one of them," I lie. "She had to go to the hospital."

I wish that was what happened, and I remember Grandmother telling me you can sin with your thoughts—that thinking something is almost as bad as actually doing it. If that's true, I've sinned as badly as the rest of them. I really wanted to punch Erin.

"Oh, Sofia." Riley steps in front of me, grabbing my shoulders. She pulls me into a hug, running a hand along the back of my head. "You must've felt so alone," she says, quietly enough that I'm sure I'm the only one who can hear her. "But you're with us now," Riley continues. "Right where you're supposed to be."

For a second it's easy to forget the real reason we're here and that Brooklyn is tied up in the corner. Then Riley squeezes me, and her embrace is just tight enough that I can't tell whether it's meant to be comforting—or a warning. When she pulls away she doesn't look at me again. Instead she turns to Brooklyn, her eyes narrowed.

"We've all humbled ourselves before God," she says, taking a few steps forward. She kneels on the floor again, this time so close that her knees press against Brooklyn's frayed jeans.

"What about you?" Riley grabs the duct tape covering Brooklyn's mouth and tears it away. Brooklyn gasps, and her head lolls down to her chest. I cringe at the angry red stripe left across her face.

Riley grabs Brooklyn's chin, forcing her to meet her eyes. Some of Brooklyn's smudged eyeliner comes off on Riley's fingers. She takes a ragged, raspy breath that sounds so painful my entire chest aches.

"Are you ready to confess?" Riley asks.

For a long moment Brooklyn won't lift her eyes from the floor. She blinks rapidly, like she's fighting back tears. This is it, I realize. This is all Riley wanted. Maybe she isn't going to perform the exorcism at all—she just wants Brooklyn to admit what she did.

Finally, Brooklyn looks up at Riley. Lips trembling, she opens her mouth.

And spits in Riley's face.

"Go to hell," she says.

# CHAPTER NINE

Riley wipes Brooklyn's spit from her cheek with the back of her hand. I expect her face to twist in fury, but she just stares ahead with glassy eyes, her mouth a thin, hard line. I don't see any sign of the girl I thought I knew—this Riley seems to be missing some key ingredient to make her human. She drinks from the wine bottle, then runs her tongue over her lips.

"How does it feel, bitch?" Brooklyn throws herself against her ropes, making the pillar she's tied to groan. She spits again, this time spraying Riley's foot. "I should baptize you in the name of *Satan*."

Riley cocks her head to the side, reminding me of a

hawk eyeing a mouse. "Well then. We have our work cut out for us. Alexis, what's next?"

"We must pray for Brooklyn's soul. I have the passage," Alexis says. I chew on the inside of my cheek as she slips a faded sheet of paper from her Bible's pages. Even now, in the middle of all this, she looks flawless in a white cardigan covered in silver hearts and jean shorts. I take that as a good sign. She wouldn't have dressed nicely if she thought things were going to get violent.

"Then I'll draw the demon forth." Riley picks up the bottle of holy water.

"Sofia, I need you." Riley holds her free hand out to me. When I don't immediately take it, she grabs my hand and weaves her fingers through mine, pulling me closer. "We can face the demon together. Your strength will be my strength."

I try to meet Riley's eyes, looking for some flicker of the Riley I like, the Riley I thought was my friend. Because of the position of the lamp, her eyes are in shadow and it's her smile that's illuminated. It twists into a smirk.

"Have some faith," she says to me. She grabs Grace's hand and brings her closer into the circle.

Alexis begins to read. "We exorcise you, impure one, you satanic power." Her clear, steady voice fills the cold corners of the basement. I want to pull my hand away from Riley's, but when I move, she squeezes tighter.

"Be humble under the powerful hand of God," Alexis says. I shift my attention back to her, wondering where she found the ridiculous passage she's reading. It sounds like something from a bad horror movie.

Alexis's voice grows louder. "Tremble and flee!" She glances up from the Bible and studies Brooklyn's face, like she's expecting her to start writhing on the floor or for smoke to pour out of her mouth.

But Brooklyn just lifts an eyebrow. "Did you find that on Wikipedia?" she asks, snickering.

"Yeah, where did you get that, Lexie?" Grace asks, frowning.

"It's the official prayer for a ritual exorcism," Alexis says.

Brooklyn laughs even harder. "I don't know why I was worried," she says. "Clearly you all are pros."

"Stop it," Riley snaps. "It doesn't matter where the passage came from. What we say isn't as important as what we believe."

Riley tips the bottle of holy water over Brooklyn's head. The water dribbles from the bottle, and Brooklyn flinches when it hits her, then blinks and stares at Riley.

She tilts her head so the remaining water pours over her face. She shakes her hair out, like a dog.

"Is this so I'll be ready for the wet T-shirt portion of the night?" she asks. Riley tightens her grip on the bottle, her smile hardening.

"She's making fun of us," Riley says. "Sof, hand me the salt."

I don't move. Riley glares at me.

"The sooner you help, the sooner all this can be over."

"Fine." I pull my fingers from Riley's grip. Brooklyn's right. Riley's not a professional—she's just a pissed-off teenage girl. Locking us in here was messed up, but this is just a hazing ritual, something to show Brooklyn who the alpha bitch is. I grab the jar of salt from the floor, thrusting it into Riley's hands. Most girls would just start a burn book.

Water drips from Brooklyn's hair.

"Keep going," Riley urges, and Alexis clears her throat.

"From the snares of the devil, free us, Lord," she continues, a little less enthusiastically than before.

Riley pours the salt in her hand and throws it. I flinch when the salt hits Brooklyn's face, but she squeezes her eyes shut and turns, so it mostly hits her hair. A few tiny white crystals cling to her wet cheeks and the corner of her mouth. Brooklyn runs her tongue along her lips.

"Next time get me some tequila and a lime to go with that," she says. I bite back a smile.

"Heathen," Riley hisses. She pours another handful of salt into her palm and whips it into Brooklyn's face. This time it catches her in the nose and mouth. Brooklyn swears under her breath, trying to blink the salt from her eyes. Riley throws another handful at her, and then another. When the jar is almost empty, she drops to the floor, her knees inches from Brooklyn's.

"This isn't enough for you, is it?" Riley wraps her fingers in Brooklyn's hair and yanks her head back, forcing her to look up. The corners of Brooklyn's eyes crinkle.

"Riley." I take a step toward her. This isn't funny anymore. Even Alexis stops reading.

"This isn't how we're supposed to do it," Alexis says, her voice wavering for the first time. The defiance fades from Brooklyn's eyes.

"Can't you see what she's doing?" Riley says. "She's laughing at us."

Riley releases Brooklyn's hair roughly and stands. Her eyes dart to the cross hanging from Alexis's neck. I'm the only one watching Brooklyn, and I see her square her shoulders and jerk her hands apart to loosen the ropes. I want to help her, but when I take a step toward her, Brooklyn moves her head back and forth, then looks pointedly at the staircase. I frown, but I understand what she's trying to tell me. We're locked down here and it's three against one. I can't afford to challenge the others yet.

"We need something stronger," Riley says, leveling her gaze on Alexis's necklace. "*That*. Alexis, let me borrow your cross."

Alexis hands me her Bible without a word. She finds the chain at her neck and fumbles with the clasp. The cross drops into her hand. She holds it out for Riley.

Riley lifts the cross by its chain. "Thanks, Lexie," she says. Riley lets the cross swing, pendulum-like, before Brooklyn's eyes.

"I exorcize you in the name of the Father, the Son, and the Holy Spirit," she says. They're almost the same words she used to baptize me.

Brooklyn watches the cross sway. Her angry red eyes flick back to Riley. Riley's expression tightens. She pulls back her arm and whips the cross over Brooklyn's face. The chain flashes through the air, landing with a smack. The cross cut deep into Brooklyn's cheek, leaving a thin red line across her skin. A single drop of blood oozes down her face, like a tear.

I take a step back. "God," I say under my breath. Any hope I had that this might not get violent drains away. We have to get out of here. Now.

"Let's try this again," Riley says.

Suddenly Brooklyn shifts her weight to the side and whips her bound legs out from under her, ramming a combat boot into Riley's shin. Riley slams into the concrete, her wrist twisting beneath her body when she hits the floor. The cross clatters out of her hand.

"Bitch!" Riley sweeps the hair from her face and

pushes herself onto all fours, wincing as she eases weight onto her wrist. Grace moves to help, but Brooklyn slams her feet into Riley again, this time striking her in the ribs. Riley collapses into Alexis, and the two of them stumble to the floor, knocking over a tea candle. The flame sputters and dies.

If it weren't for the lock on the basement door, this would be the perfect time to run. The muscles in my legs tense, but I hold myself still. By the time I think of tackling Riley and stealing the key, she's already standing again.

Brooklyn's sharp laughter fills the basement. Her eyes flicker with red light, and even though it must be the reflection of the candlelight, they look like they're glowing. "Riley, I think it's working!" she shouts. "I think I'm saved!"

"Oh my god." Grace bunches her hands near her mouth. "Alexis, your sweater!"

A curl of smoke twists away from Alexis's back, growing thicker as it drifts toward the ceiling. Orange and blue flames lick at the tiny white hearts along her sweater's hem.

"Shit, Lexie, you're on fire!" I say.

Alexis twists around, screaming when the fire catches on her sleeve. She tries to pull the sweater off, but her hands shake so badly she can't seem to work the buttons.

I grab her arm and yank at the cardigan, not caring when the buttons pop off and clatter to the ground. Alexis flings it away from her body as the fire climbs up the sleeve. The sweater lands on another candle a few feet away, still crackling. The flames eat at a tiny pearl button, and the smoke around it fills the basement with a hazy gray cloud.

Grace mutters a string of curses under her breath. She pulls her sweatshirt up over her mouth and stomps the fire out with her sneaker. The fire dies, but the smoke remains. Grace wraps her arms around Alexis's shoulders, pulling her into a hug.

"Shh, you're fine," Grace whispers.

Brooklyn leans against the pillar and takes a shaky breath. "I needed a cigarette, but I guess this will do."

Riley's cheeks are flushed red and her hair is more disheveled than I've ever seen it before. She approaches Brooklyn slowly. I dig my teeth into my lower lip, wanting so badly for Brooklyn to kick Riley again, for her to go down long enough for me to steal the key and get out of here. But Riley stops when she reaches Brooklyn's combat boots.

"You look scared, Ri," Brooklyn says. "I thought demons were supposed to cower before your God, not the other way around."

I take a deep breath and calmly search the room for

something I could use to pick the padlock at the top of the stairs—or even a weapon. I'm past pretending to be on Riley's side, past letting this play out and hoping no one gets hurt. This stops now.

"Alexis, get me the knife," Riley says, and I freeze. Nothing down here is strong enough to use against the knife. Alexis slides it off the floor. The sound of metal dragging over concrete cuts through the basement.

Riley grabs the knife from Alexis. She runs a perfectly manicured nail along the length of the blade. When she reaches the tip, she presses the flesh of her finger into it, drawing a tiny bead of blood. The blood winds around her finger.

"Good," she says, taking a step closer to Brooklyn. "It's sharp."

"Holding a big knife doesn't make you scary," Brooklyn says. A smile tugs at her lips. "I have to believe you've got the balls to use it."

"You don't believe I'll use this?" Riley asks. Brooklyn starts to shift her legs, but Riley drops onto them before she can lift them off the ground. She slams the knife handle into the side of Brooklyn's knee, just below the cap.

Brooklyn's mouth forms a perfect O, and her skin turns white. Her face crumples, and she lets out a strangled cry.

Alexis walks behind Brooklyn and yanks her head back, exposing the pale, fragile skin at her neck. Riley lifts the knife and pushes the tip of the blade to Brooklyn's neck. She turns it as she speaks, twisting the sharp point farther into Brooklyn's skin. Brooklyn cringes and tries to pull away, but the pillar behind her head blocks her in.

"Tell me: Are you scared yet?" Riley asks.

# CHAPTER TEN

Riley pushes the knife closer to Brooklyn's throat. I try not to think about how easily she could rip it open. She'll draw blood if either of them moves. I can practically feel the hate radiating off Riley's skin. Maybe she does want to help Brooklyn, but that's not all she wants. She wants her to pay.

"Wait!" The word flies from my mouth before I can think about what I'm doing. Silence follows, and now they're all looking at me, expecting an explanation. I clear my throat and take a hesitant step toward Riley. "Let me try."

I know Brooklyn's sin. Maybe I can get her to

admit it without hurting her. Riley considers me with an icy expression, almost as if she can see past my skin and bones, to all the parts I want to keep hidden from her. Then, as though she flipped a switch, her face lights up.

"Of course," she says. "You should be the one to get her to confess."

She pushes the knife to my palm, and I wrap my fingers around it. My skin tingles where it touches the wooden handle. Riley takes me by the shoulders and pulls me close, kissing me on the cheek.

"Make us proud," she says. Her lips leave behind a damp spot that burns into my skin like acid, but I don't wipe it away. Maybe it's sick, but I *do* want to make Riley proud, even after everything.

"Brooklyn," I say, forcing myself to meet Brooklyn's gaze, "I know what you did at the party. I saw you. If you just admit it, we can all go home."

"What did I do, Sofia?" Brooklyn asks. She blinks at me, her dark eyes filled with hate. "Enlighten me."

"You were in the hot tub with Josh," I say. "You were . . ." I don't want to describe the possessive way she mashed her mouth against Josh's and wrapped her arms around his neck, so I let the rest of my sentence trail off, hoping the others can fill in the blanks.

"Ri, why didn't you tell us?" Grace says.

"I don't think I wanted to admit it," Riley whispers. "I . . ."

"Wait," Brooklyn interrupts. "You think I screwed your boyfriend?" She pulls her battered leg closer to her body, and her boots scrape against the floor. "I never touched that preppy asshole."

"Brooklyn, I'm trying to . . ." *Help you*, I'd wanted to say. But I press my lips together, cutting myself off.

Riley touches my arm. "She just wants to piss us off," she says. "But I have ways of finding the truth."

She pulls a cell phone out of her back pocket. It's covered in duct tape, and someone drew a tiny picture of a kitten with vampire teeth on the back in thick black Sharpie.

"What are you doing with my phone?" Brooklyn asks. "Did you think me and Josh were sending each other dirty text messages?"

"If you were, you deleted them," Riley answers. Her eyes have that glow to them again, the same glow they had when she first brought me here to see Brooklyn tied up. "I guess I'll just have to write some new ones. If you're not going to admit you've been screwing my boyfriend, I'll get him to do it for you."

I stare at the phone, wanting to grab it from Riley's hands and call the police.

"*What are you doing?*" Riley reads as she types the message. "*I'm lonely.*"

She hesitates for a beat, then taps the screen with her thumb. "Send," she says. She slides the phone back into her pocket and crouches in front of Brooklyn again.

"Now, what should we do while we wait for a response?" she asks, unbending a finger from Brooklyn's fist. She takes the knife from my hands before I can stop her and slides the tip of it beneath Brooklyn's fingernail. A phantom pain shoots through all my fingers at once. "How about we play a game? Either you admit your sins, or I do your nails."

Brooklyn glances down at the knife, then back up at Riley.

"Go to hell," she says through clenched teeth.

"That didn't sound like a sin to me," Riley says, and she drives the knife beneath Brooklyn's fingernail.

Brooklyn throws her head against the pillar and releases a desperate, animalistic scream. I close my eyes, and, again, I see Riley wedge the knife beneath Brooklyn's fingernail and shove it forward; I hear the sick pop of the nail separating from Brooklyn's finger. I start to heave, but I force it down. I can't fall apart now. I have to get Brooklyn out of here.

I open my eyes in time to see Brooklyn's tiny black fingernail fall from Riley's knife and drop to the floor. Brooklyn's screams dissolve into shaky sobs, her chest rising and falling rapidly. I stare at the bloody clump on the concrete as Riley unpeels another finger from Brooklyn's fist and slides the tip of her knife just beneath the nail.

"Riley, let's air this place out," I interrupt before Riley pushes the knife any farther under Brooklyn's fingernail. The smoke is thick enough to agitate the back of my throat. Riley's shoulders stiffen and I freeze, certain she heard the fear in my voice. Any second she'll turn the knife on me.

Then her shoulders sag, and she wipes the sweat from her forehead with the back of her hand. "Yeah," she says. "Let's go upstairs."

Grace and Alexis crowd around Riley as they make their way to the door. I let them walk ahead of me, hesitating at the bottom of the stairs.

Now that she's alone, Brooklyn collapses against the wooden pillar and her chest rises and falls in quick succession, like she's going to start hyperventilating. She moves her leg and a spasm of pain shoots across her face.

Riley digs the dead bolt key out of her pocket, her hair covering her face like a veil. Grace and Alexis huddle behind her, whispering in hushed, sympathetic voices. It sounds like they're talking about Josh, but I'm not really listening.

I could untie Brooklyn, and then it would be three

against two. Brooklyn's hurt, but we might still be able to get past them.

I step back from the stairs, rolling my foot from the ball to the heel so the soles of my sneakers don't squeak against the floor.

Alexis pats Riley on the shoulder. "It's better this way," she says. I try to breathe normally, but every time I inhale, my mouth fills with smoke and I have to struggle not to cough. "At least now you know what kind of guy he is."

I duck around the concrete wall and race across the basement to kneel next to Brooklyn. She stares straight ahead, like she can't see me.

"What are you doing?" she hisses, her voice barely a whisper. I grab the rope binding her to the pillar and try to pull the knot apart with my fingers.

"I'm getting you out of here." I say the words directly into her ear so they don't echo across the basement.

"Riley's ruthless. If she catches you, she'll tie you up, too," Brooklyn whispers. The ropes slip in my fingers. Shaking now, I search the basement for something I can use to help pull them apart.

"I was lucky Sofia saw them," Riley says, her voice drifting down the staircase. I ignore her, grabbing a ball-point pen sticking from the pages of Alexis's Bible. I try to jerk Brooklyn's knots loose.

"Sofia?" Riley calls. There's a moment of silence, and my body goes cold, my fingers frozen on the ropes. The stairs creak as Riley starts down.

"Damn it," I whisper, digging the pen deeper into the knots. Brooklyn twists around to face me.

"Go," she says. "Our only chance is if she thinks she can trust you. Otherwise we're both screwed."

"Sof, what are you doing?" Riley calls down the stairs. There's another groan of wood, and I hear Alexis and Grace whispering as they head back down to the basement with her. I'm so close. The knots will give at any moment. I twist the pen against the ropes, and it slips from my sweaty fingers, clattering to the floor.

"Shit," I hiss.

The footsteps hesitate, and someone mutters, "What was that?"

Brooklyn glances at the staircase, and a muscle in her jaw tightens.

"Stab me." Her eyes shift down to the pen on the floor. *"What?"*

"Sofia, she *has* to trust you," Brooklyn insists. "It's our only way out." I wipe my hands on my pants and pick up the pen. My fingers tremble as I lift the pen to Brooklyn's leg. There's no way I can do this. Riley's feet slap against the basement floor—any second she'll turn the corner and see me.

"Do it!" Brooklyn says. A candle sparks behind me, turning Brooklyn's eyes red. They look like they're glowing again. I nervously drop the pen, and it clatters to the floor again, rolling next to Brooklyn's fingers. I reach for it, but Brooklyn grabs it first.

Without hesitating, she wraps her fingers around the pen and drives it into her leg.

"Shit!" Brooklyn screams. A dark circle of blood appears on her jean shorts. Tears spring to her eyes, and she throws her head back against the pillar, sobbing. She pushes the pen into my hand, and I immediately wrap my fingers around it, trying not to feel ill. I can't bring myself to look down at the blood staining the pen's tip.

"Oh my god!" Riley shouts. She's at my side now and watches the blood spread across Brooklyn's leg, her eyes bright—proud.

"She tried to escape," I lie. "As soon as you went for the staircase, she started pulling at her ropes."

Riley presses her lips into a thin line and squeezes my shoulder. It simultaneously comforts and disgusts me. "I knew we could count on you."

# CHAPTER ELEVEN

My grandmother told me about an exorcism she went to once. She was very young, at a small country church in Mexico. A five-year-old boy was brought before the congregation. He'd cut the skin on his arms to ribbons using a straight pin he found in his mother's sewing kit, and he spoke in a language no one knew. The priest spent the entire day dousing the boy with holy water and saying prayer after prayer for his salvation. The day grew late, and most of the congregation left. But my grandmother and her mother stayed and prayed over their rosaries to give the priest and the boy strength.

My grandmother's voice—strong and deep before she got sick—always got quiet when she told the next part of the story:

"The boy, he *tembla*—trembles—and he cries in pain," she'd say in her shaky English, grabbing and motioning with her hands as she spoke, like she was trying to pull the story from the air. "His eyes glow red, and he falls to the ground, and he screams. When he opened his eyes, *mija*, they don't glow anymore. We knew he was saved. Free."

I turn my grandmother's words over in my head while Brooklyn howls in pain. I think of how her leg gave way beneath the pen's sharp tip and my hands quiver. Footsteps echo across the floor.

"Oh my god. What happened?" Alexis asks. Grace hovers behind her, keeping to the farthest corner of the basement.

"Brooklyn almost got away, but Sofia stopped her," Riley explains. "We can't stop now, not when she's weakening. Let's pray."

Alexis reaches for Riley's hand, but Riley takes mine instead. "Alexis, can you pray over Brooklyn? I want Sof next to me."

Jealousy flashes across Alexis's face, but it's gone in an instant. "Of course," she says. "Whatever you think is best."

Riley tightens her hand around mine. She sees me as

one of them now. Brooklyn whimpers, and I glance up, meeting her eyes. Even now her pupils seem to glow red.

Grandmother's low, gravelly voice echoes through my head.

*"The boy, his eyes glow red, and he falls to the ground, and he screams. . . ."*

Cringing, I look away. It's just the candles, nothing more.

Alexis closes her eyes and starts speaking in another language. *"Pater noster, qui es in caelis,"* she whispers, swaying. The Latin sounds strange when spoken in her Southern accent.

Brooklyn writhes on the floor below her. Her eyelids flicker open, but she rolls her pupils so far back that all I see are the whites. I'm reminded, again, of the boy who shook and trembled while my grandmother and her mother recited the Lord's Prayer in that empty church. Then Brooklyn snickers, breaking the spell.

"She's screwing with us," Riley says. She grabs the backpack and pulls out a pack of matches. A cold finger of fear traces down my spine.

"What are you going to do?" I ask.

"Trust me," she says. She strikes a match, and for a moment we're all quiet. The sulfur lights, shooting blue sparks from the tip before the fire deepens to a flickering red-orange. Riley turns the match in her fingers, and its flame reflects in her dark eyes.

She throws it at Brooklyn.

The match lands on Brooklyn's bare leg, just below her frayed cutoff shorts. All at once her face seems to fold in on itself. She sucks in a sharp breath, shaking her leg wildly to get the match off her skin. It falls to the concrete and dies, leaving only the smell of burning pennies.

"Your turn." Riley takes my hand and places the pack of matches on my palm. I hesitate. The cardboard box seems heavy, even though I know it's practically weightless. "Is there a problem?"

"No," I say too quickly. I slowly remove a single match from the pack and light it against the sulfur strip on the bottom of the lid. I run through every option I can think of, trying to figure a way around this, an excuse, a distraction—anything. I search every dusty corner, but there's nothing. No plan, no other options.

The match's flame flickers, first blue then orange.

*I have to get out of here*, I tell myself, but the words don't have much power. Riley's testing me, and I have to pass if I stand a chance.

The flame creeps slowly down the match. My fingers tremble so badly it almost goes out. I lift my hand and toss the match into the air. Luckily, my shaking fingers cause the match to land on the concrete next to Brooklyn instead of on her bare skin.

"So close, Sof," Riley says, but she isn't watching anymore. She picks the knife up off the ground.

Alexis starts chanting again. *"Sanctificetur nomen tuum . . ."*

Next to me, Grace closes her eyes and lifts her hands to the ceiling in prayer.

"Again, Sofia," Riley says as she kneels before Brooklyn. This time, when I light the match, I let the flame burn down until it's almost to my fingers. It dies in midair before hitting Brooklyn's skin, and I feel an instant rush of relief.

Brooklyn barely notices when the blackened match drops on her leg. Her eyes are on Riley's knife.

"More threats?" she asks in a choked voice. "That's getting old."

Riley turns the knife so its blade catches the candlelight. "I read about this method of exorcism called bleeding," she explains. "If you harm the host body enough, it scares the demon away."

Riley presses the knife into Brooklyn's exposed thigh and pulls the blade toward her knee. She moves the knife so slowly that I hear the skin rip seconds before a thin red line of blood appears on Brooklyn's leg.

Brooklyn presses her eyes closed and her jaw clenches, but she doesn't scream. Blood bubbles up just above her knee and winds around her leg.

"Riley," I say. Another match burns to life, but I'm so distracted that it dies in my hand, stinging my fingers. I drop it with a start.

"Don't worry, the cuts aren't deep," Riley says. "We don't want to kill her—we just want the demon scared."

Riley pulls the knife across Brooklyn's opposite thigh, just as slowly. I imagine the knife biting the flesh on my thighs, tearing my skin. It stings.

Brooklyn's mouth falls open in a wordless sob. Her chest rises and falls rapidly, and tears cut down her face, leaving behind murky gray trails of eyeliner. Next, Riley drags the blade over Brooklyn's shins—first the left, then the right. Blood drips to the floor.

Alexis falls to her knees, chanting louder. *"Adveniat regnum tuum!"*

Riley stands, the bloody knife still clenched in one hand. She brushes the hair from her forehead, leaving a smudge of red above her eyebrow.

"Sof, could you hand me the salt?" Riley asks, wiping her bloody fingers on her jeans. "I don't want to get blood everywhere."

My body moves before I tell it to, like someone else has control of my arms and legs. Grace is still swaying, her arms in the air above her, her eyes clenched shut. I walk past her and crouch next to the faded backpack lying against the wall, finding a bag of salt in the front pocket.

When I turn back around, the pool of blood beneath Brooklyn has oozed beneath Riley's bare feet. She doesn't notice, and when she walks toward me, her toes leave bloody prints on the concrete.

"Thanks," she says, taking the salt from my hands. Riley pushes a lock of my hair back behind one ear. I feel something wet and warm against my cheek. Brooklyn's blood.

Riley opens the bag of salt and pours a handful into her palm. I want to close my eyes, like Grace, so I don't have to see what she's about to do. But fear keeps me from turning my head or pressing my eyes shut. It's the same fear that keeps me from telling Riley to stop or trying to wrestle her knife away. I don't want to be next.

Riley crouches in front of Brooklyn again. Blood soaks through her jeans where she kneels. She takes Brooklyn by the chin and forces the salt past her clenched lips.

Brooklyn's eyes fly open. She tries to pull her head away, but Alexis comes up behind her and grabs her by the hair to hold her steady. Riley covers Brooklyn's mouth with both her hands.

Brooklyn whips her head to one side, then the other. Alexis tightens her grip on her hair, and Riley pushes her hands up against her face, until Brooklyn can't move at all.

"I'll let go when you admit your sins," Riley says. Brooklyn goes still. Her eyelids flutter, but they don't close.

"Are you ready to submit before the Lord?"

Brooklyn nods, and, slowly, Riley leans back. Alexis pulls her hands out of Brooklyn's hair, a few spiky bleached-blond strands still clenched between her fingers.

Brooklyn heaves forward, vomiting the salt onto the floor. Still bent over, she lets out a low sob, then spits to get all the salt out of her mouth.

"Well?" Riley says. Brooklyn shakes her head and mutters something too quietly for the rest of us to hear. Riley grabs her by the hair and pulls her head up.

"I didn't hear you."

Brooklyn inhales shakily. Riley leans in closer.

A tense, hushed silence stretches between us. Wind presses in against the window. The fabric on Grace's sweatshirt rustles as she moves her arms. A brief, faint hope sparks in my chest.

*Please. Please just let this be over.*

Brooklyn lifts her dark, hate-filled eyes to Riley and parts her lips. Blood spatters her nose and drips down over her teeth.

She lunges forward, grabbing a chunk of Riley's face between her teeth.

Riley's horrified scream cuts the silence. Brooklyn's lips are coated with red when she pulls away. She spits, and a blood-covered chunk of skin slides across the concrete floor.

# CHAPTER TWELVE

"You fucking bitch!" Riley stumbles away from Brooklyn, clutching her face with both hands. Blood appears in the cracks between her fingers.

"Riley, oh my god!" Alexis tries to pry Riley's bunched fist from her face, but Riley shoves her away.

"Get me a bandage!" she screams. Behind her, Brooklyn licks the blood from her lips. Her eyes shift to the staircase, but this time I don't need her to tell me what to do.

"We have to get to a bathroom," I say. I go to Riley's side and gently pry her fingers from her face. She moves her hand just long enough for me to see the mangled, bloody skin beneath. Brooklyn's teeth left a perfect indentation on her cheek. "It'll get infected if you don't wash it."

Riley's fingers tremble. She nods, letting me steer her toward the staircase.

"I think I saw Band-Aids in the kitchen," Grace adds.

Alexis tightens Brooklyn's ropes. "These should hold this time," she says, then follows us up the stairs.

I keep my expression emotionless as Riley slips her free hand into her pocket and pulls out the key to the basement door, hoping she can't read in my face how badly I want to rip it from her fingers. After she unlocks the dead bolt, Riley grabs my hand and squeezes.

"Once we clean off the blood you won't see a thing," I lie. I wouldn't be surprised if she had a scar on her face for the rest of her life. Alexis narrows her eyes at me but says nothing.

Once upstairs, I let Alexis take Riley's arm as Grace leads the way to the bathroom. I hold the door open while they all filter inside.

"I'll find the Band-Aids," I say. Riley nods, but the bathroom mirror distracts her. She mutters a curse and leans over the sink, gingerly patting the tender skin around her wound. For the first time since getting here, nobody's watching me.

I slip down the hall, into the kitchen. Dust coats

the countertops and cobwebs stretch across the ceiling. No back door like I'd been hoping, but there's a single window on the far wall. I lean over the sink to reach it, but another row of crooked nails jutting out of the sill keeps me from trying to pry it open.

A long, colorful string of curse words flies through my head. Riley must've nailed every single window shut. I lean back again and wipe the dust from the window ledge on the seat of my pants, then start opening cupboards and drawers. There might be a spare key around here, or at least something I could use as a weapon.

But the cupboards are mostly empty, with cobwebs stretching across the corners. There's a wineglass on the highest shelf. Standing on my tiptoes, I pull it down. It's plastic, not glass—no use as a weapon. Bright red lipstick, like the kind Brooklyn wears, smudges around the lip, and the bottom is stained red from wine that never got rinsed out. I set the glass back inside the cupboard and close the door. Kneeling, I open the cupboard below, but all I find is half a loaf of bread and a plastic jar of peanut butter.

"Sofia, we found the Band-Aids," Grace yells from the bathroom, startling me. "They were in here, under the sink."

If they're bandaging Riley up already, then they're almost done. Sighing, I stare through the dirty glass in the window above the sink. There's no yard behind the house, just a long stretch of upturned dirt bordered by thick trees, their leaves already turning orange and brown.

I wonder what's on the other side of those trees. More abandoned houses and empty lots? Or could there be a road, businesses—civilization?

Something moves in the yard beyond the dirty glass.

I see it from the corner of my eye and glance up. It's a man—homeless from the looks of it. He wears a black T-shirt and sweatpants, tattered and at least three sizes too big, and he's holding a bottle concealed by a brown paper bag.

He stumbles through the trees. Any second he'll disappear. I lean over the sink, lifting a hand to bang on the glass. My voice catches in my throat as I smack my fist against the window. The man cocks his head toward the house. I open my mouth to yell.

"Sofia?"

I clench my mouth shut and whirl around. Riley's right behind me. She glances at the window.

"There was a bug," I lie, lowering my hand. "A cockroach."

Riley wrinkles her nose. "Gross. Didn't you hear us? We found the Band-Aids."

She motions to the flesh-colored bandages on her

face. They make an X over her left cheek. I want to turn back to the window and see if the homeless man is still there, but I can't do that with Riley standing in front of me. Riley crosses the kitchen and leans against the sink.

"I know you feel uneasy about what we're doing," she says. She makes it sound like I'm nervous about sneaking out at night or going skinny-dipping.

"I wanted to show you this to help you understand." Riley pulls a folded piece of paper from her pocket and hands it to me.

It's a newspaper clipping. I unfold it and read the headline. BELOVED TEACHER KILLED IN ACCIDENT. Just below is a photograph of an older man with thick white hair and dark, deeply lined skin.

I frown, scanning the first lines of the article.

*Adams High School geography teacher and drama coach Carlton Willis died at 8 PM last night when he fell from a ladder in the school gymnasium. He leaves behind his wife, Julianna Willis . . .*

Something familiar tugs at my brain, but I can't figure out what it is. "What does this have to do with Brooklyn?"

"Mr. Willis used to lead a Bible study after school." Riley wraps her fingers around the edge of the sink. "Grace and Brooklyn were in his last period geography together last year. Grace says Brooklyn *hated* Mr. Willis.

One day, Brooklyn was chanting in the back of his class. It was really creepy and disruptive, and Mr. Willis kicked her out. But before she left she threw her textbook at him. Grace says she broke a window. Mr. Willis swore he was going to have her expelled—maybe even arrested."

Despite myself, I'm curious. "So what happened next?"

"Nothing. That was the night Mr. Willis had his accident."

"Accident . . ." I glance back down at the black-and-white photograph on the clipping. Something on Mr. Willis's hand catches my eye: a thick, gold wedding ring. I move my eyes back over the obituary, and once again I stop at the last line in the first paragraph: *He leaves behind wife, Julianna Willis . . .*

CARLTON & JULIANNA 1979.

"His ring," I say, pointing at the picture. "Brooklyn . . ."

"Brooklyn wears it around her neck," Riley finishes for me. She brushes a strand of hair off her forehead. "Like a trophy."

I shake my head. This is insane. "But *why?*"

"Because she's the one who killed him," Riley said. "Because she's evil. That's why we have to stop her."

\* \* \*

I consider Riley's story as we make our way back down the stairs. First there was the skinned cat beneath the bleachers, and now a teacher. Could Riley be spreading more lies? Or is Brooklyn actually dangerous?

Brooklyn's eyes are closed when we get down to the basement, but they flicker open at the sound of our footsteps.

"Back for more?" she asks.

Riley's expression hardens. She lifts a hand to the bandages on her cheek. "Don't we have any more wine?" she says.

Grace pulls a new bottle out of the backpack and hands it to her. I expect Riley to smash it against the wall and attack Brooklyn with the broken glass. But she just twists off the screw top and drinks, watching Brooklyn over the mouth of the bottle.

The cell phone in her back pocket vibrates, and Riley lowers the bottle of wine. All at once it's like the air in the basement thickens. Riley pulls out the phone and taps the screen. She shifts her eyes up to Brooklyn.

"It's from Josh," she says. "He wrote . . ." Riley hesitates, and every muscle in her body tenses. *"Need some company?"*

Any hope I had that this might be over vanishes. Riley tosses Brooklyn's cell phone, and it skitters across the floor. She drops to her knees, straddling Brooklyn's bound legs.

"Whore," she spits, and whips a hand across Brooklyn's

face. Brooklyn's head smacks against the wooden pillar behind her. I cringe and look away, my gaze falling on the butcher knife half wedged beneath the backpack at Grace's feet. No one else seems to remember that it's there.

"Admit it!" Riley screams. I shift my feet to the left, edging slowly closer to the knife.

"Fine!" Brooklyn shouts. She spits blood onto the concrete and stretches out her jaw. "You want me to admit my fucking sins? I did it, okay? I slept with your boyfriend. And you know what the best part is? We'd come here, to this house, and we'd drink your wine, and he'd screw me on your sleeping bag."

Riley's face is empty, expressionless, like she didn't hear a word of Brooklyn's confession. Without even blinking, she slaps her again. I drop to a crouch next to the knife and slide it out from beneath the backpack. Riley stands and starts to pace.

"Give me that," she says, stopping directly in front of me. Before I can say a word, Riley rips the butcher knife from my hand.

"Riley." I stand, no longer thinking about what's smart or what will convince Riley I'm on her side. If Josh is what sent Riley off the rails in the first place, who knows what she'll do now. I reach for the knife, but Riley holds it close to her side possessively. "Come on. She admitted her sin, there's nothing left for us to do."

Riley shakes her head. "That wasn't her only sin." She crouches near Brooklyn again, this time grabbing her hand. "Hand me the Bible, Lexie," she says.

Alexis doesn't answer her. Her glassy eyes are fixed on the far wall.

"Lexie!" Riley yells, and Alexis flinches. "Hand me the Bible."

Alexis takes the Bible out of the backpack and passes it to Riley. "Dirty sinner," she mutters as Riley slides the Bible beneath Brooklyn's hand, then spreads her fingers out flat on its cover.

Brooklyn lifts her face. Black eyeliner seeps into the corners of her eyes and smudges around her nose. Her mouth is rimmed in blood. She tries to pull her hand away, but Riley holds it tight, pressing Brooklyn's fingers down flat with her palm. She positions the knife over the tip of Brooklyn's pinkie.

"You fucking psycho!" Brooklyn screams. She kicks and squirms, fighting against the ropes binding her in place. "Just let me go!"

"Guys, help me hold her down," Riley says. Alexis immediately moves behind Brooklyn and grabs her shoulders so she can't throw herself against the ropes anymore. Grace hesitates, then crouches beside Riley and grabs Brooklyn's wrist.

Riley moves both hands to the knife.

"Okay, okay!" Brooklyn shouts, fear slurring her words. "I killed the cat beneath the bleachers. It was wandering around my apartment complex, so I drowned it in my bathtub. Then I skinned it with this pocket-knife I stole from a kid at school. Is that what you want to hear?"

"I don't care what depraved thing you did with that cat." Riley rocks the knife over Brooklyn's finger and Brooklyn cringes from the sting of the blade. "Tell me about Mr. Willis."

Brooklyn shakes her head. "He had an accident. What do you want me to say?"

Riley presses down on the knife. There's a crunch as the blade slices through skin and nail and digs into the leather cover of the Bible beneath Brooklyn's fingers. My breath catches in my throat, and I clench my eyes shut so I don't see the tip of Brooklyn's pinkie roll off the Bible and land on the floor with a sticky thud.

Brooklyn's screaming vibrates through the basement and echoes off the walls. When I open my eyes again, Riley has another finger stretched across the Bible. Blood drips onto the floor, leaking from Brooklyn's bloody pinkie. Riley didn't cut off that much skin. She slid her knife right below the nail, taking only a millimeter of Brooklyn's finger at most. Still, I can't stop staring at the bloody stump she left behind.

I back up until I feel the cold concrete wall behind me. Sweat drenches my entire body. I don't know what's worse—the stories Brooklyn's telling or what Riley's doing to get her to admit to them.

"Tell me about Mr. Willis," Riley says again.

"I killed him, too!" Brooklyn yells, struggling to pull her hand away. "I waited for him in the auditorium. I wanted it to look like an accident, so when he got out the ladder and started climbing, I . . . I . . ."

"You pushed him?" Riley finishes for her. Brooklyn presses her lips together and nods.

"Yes. Yes, I pushed him," Brooklyn screams. "Are you happy now, you psycho?"

I taste sour bile at the back of my throat. I try to swallow, but the sharp, metallic scent of blood and the lingering smoke fill my nostrils. My stomach cramps and restricts, and acid rises in my throat. I drop to my knees and my entire body heaves, splattering vomit onto the concrete.

I look up and Brooklyn catches my eye. She slowly shakes her head and her eyes turn desperate, pained. She's lying, I realize. She's just trying to survive. I exhale in relief.

"Yes, actually, I am happy," Riley says, her lips twisting into a sneer. "Now you just have to be baptized."

# CHAPTER THIRTEEN

I work my fingers through the tangled knots binding Brooklyn to the pillar. She barely moves now, having passed out from blood loss or pain, I'm not sure. The stiff ropes scratch my skin, but they finally come loose and pull apart. *We're getting out of here*, I want to tell Brooklyn. The baptism will be easy compared with what she's already been through.

Brooklyn's eyelids flicker but stay closed. Grace wraps a wad of toilet paper around the remaining stub of her finger and secures it with a few Band-Aids. I avoid looking at the bloody tissues while she works.

"Make sure to tie up her arms and legs again." Riley

sticks a heavy wooden cross and the remaining salt and holy water into the backpack. "We're going all the way up to the second floor. Don't want her to get loose."

"Isn't there a bathroom on the first floor?" I ask. Alexis crawls around me, toward Brooklyn's legs, and starts retying the bindings at her ankles.

"Only the bathrooms on the second floor have bath-tubs," Riley says.

"Why do we need a tub?"

"You'll see." Riley's words chill me, but I say nothing. I tie the ropes at Brooklyn's wrists, leaving them loose intentionally—just in case. Alexis finishes the knot at Brooklyn's ankles and starts to giggle.

"What's so funny?" I ask her. Alexis glances up, but her eyes don't quite focus on my face.

"It's like she's not even real," she says, poking Brooklyn's limp leg. "She's like a doll."

I try not to think too hard about what she means. Riley sets the backpack down next to the wall and grabs Brooklyn's arms while Alexis and Grace take her legs. Even with the three of them lifting together, they're only able to get her a few feet off the ground. They crouch as they walk, moving slowly toward the staircase. Alexis's breathing grows heavier with every move, and Grace already looks like she might pass out. Sweat lines her forehead, and a few fuzzy strands of hair come loose from her ponytail. They stick out of her head at odd angles.

"Sof, can you blow out the candles?" Riley asks, groaning as she shifts Brooklyn's weight. One of her arms is looped around Brooklyn's torso, while Grace now holds her bound arms and shoulders. Riley's face tightens every time she takes a step back. "And grab the backpack?"

"Okay." I quickly blow out the candles on the far side of the basement and move to grab the backpack still leaning against the wall. I kneel next to it and start shoving the knife and rosary inside. Then my hand brushes against something hard and plastic. I freeze.

Brooklyn's cell phone sits next to the backpack, wedged between the strap and the wall. It must've landed back here after Riley threw it.

Nerves race up my spine. I glance over my shoulder. Riley and the others are still dragging Brooklyn up the stairs. I pick up the phone and press the power button. The screen lights up. Any fear I had that Riley might see me vanishes. Brooklyn lost a *finger*. She needs to get to the hospital.

I move my thumbs over the screen.

*911*, I type. When I press send the screen flashes a warning: 2% POWER.

I swear under my breath. Maybe a text will go through. I press the message icon, and Josh's last text pops up.

*Need company?* Josh wrote. I think of what Brooklyn said—that this is where they used to go together.

*Yeah, come to the house*, I type, praying he'll remember which house is the right one. I press send, but before I can see whether the text goes through, the screen goes black.

"Sof?" Riley calls.

"Coming." I stick the cell phone in the backpack and pull the bag over one shoulder. Riley and the others are halfway up the stairs now. I slip past them and help Riley with Brooklyn's shoulders. Relief washes over her face as I take on some of the weight.

"Maybe Grace can get the door?" I say. Riley nods.

"The key is in my side pocket."

Grace slips her hand into Riley's pocket and removes the key. She unlocks the dead bolt and pushes the door open. I focus on the text message and the possibility that Josh might be on his way now.

*He's coming*, I think. One way or another, we're getting out of here.

I breathe deeply, trying to get a better grip on Brooklyn's torso by repositioning my arms beneath her shoulder. My back aches from hunching over, and pain shoots up my calves as we shuffle across the living room and into the main hall, where a shadowy staircase leads to the second floor.

Grace helps Alexis by taking one of Brooklyn's legs, but still it's a struggle as we half pull, half carry her up the stairs. Blue veins run along Brooklyn's closed eyelids, and her skin is pale as milk. If I didn't feel her breath on the back of my arm, I'd worry she was already dead.

We pause on the staircase landing to catch our breath. Long fingers of moonlight reach through the arched window next to us and stretch over the polished wood floor. Gasping, Riley leans against the wall, holding a hand over her chest. I glance out the window next to her, hoping to see Josh's car driving toward the house. But the street is empty.

"Come on," she says, readjusting Brooklyn's weight. "We're almost there."

The second floor is less developed than the first. Cloudy plastic hangs from the ceiling, blocking off sections of unfinished wall. A paint can sits next to one of the bedroom doors, surrounded by a few empty Bud Light bottles.

The master bedroom is directly across from the staircase. Moonlight pours through the windows as we slide Brooklyn across the dark gray tile floors, leaving behind bloody smudges. It's past midnight. Soon, the moon will dip behind the far hills and the whole house will grow even darker than it is now.

The bathroom is huge. White marble stretches out

across one wall, and the largest Jacuzzi tub I've ever seen is tucked in the corner, beneath a window covered in cloudy plastic. A thin film of dust coats the porcelain double sink.

When she reaches the tub, Riley sets Brooklyn down and leans against the counter, panting. I let go of her shoulder, too, and try to set her down gently on the tile. Brooklyn groans and curls into a fetal position. Slow, shaky breaths escape her mouth.

"Sof, you have the holy water, right?" Riley leans over the tub and turns on the faucet. Nothing happens. She swears under her breath and turns the faucet off and then on again, but nothing comes out.

"Maybe we can just sprinkle Brooklyn with holy water, or . . ." I start. A churning, gurgling sound echoes below the tub, cutting me off. Thick brown water spurts from the faucet. Riley squeals and plugs the drain.

"Perfect," she says, watching the dirty brown water fill the tub.

Grace makes a face and covers her nose with her hand. "Gross."

"All things are made pure in the eyes of God," Alexis says. She stares down at the muddy brown water and giggles again. "Dirty, dirty, dirty," she whispers.

Her voice makes my skin crawl. Grace cringes as the tub fills and finally turns away—unable to watch.

On the floor, Brooklyn releases a low moan. Riley kneels next to her and pushes a sweaty strand of hair off her forehead.

"Hush, now," she says. "This will all be over soon."

Brooklyn presses her lips together and nods. Even I can't help but be comforted by Riley's words. *This will all be over soon.* Alexis leans past Riley and shuts off the faucet.

"Tub's full," she says. "Do you need help lifting her?"

Riley's eyes shift to me. "The holy water?"

"Oh, right." I pull open the backpack and dig out the now half-full bottle of holy water. I hand it to Riley, and she pours a few drops into the dirty brown sludge. She sets the bottle on the counter, then hauls Brooklyn up by the shoulders. Alexis grabs Brooklyn's arms to hold her steady.

"I baptize you in the name of the Father, the Son, and the Holy Spirit," Riley says, and shoves her face-first into the bathtub. Water drips down the side of the tub.

I hold my breath as Brooklyn struggles in the tub. I remember my own baptism, and my lungs burn all over again.

"Let her up," I say. "That's enough."

· But Riley tightens her grip, shoving Brooklyn farther below the water. "Just a few more seconds," she says.

Brooklyn pushes against Riley's hand, but Riley grits

her teeth and holds her down. Bubbles float to the surface of the murky water. I push past Grace and kneel next to the bathtub.

"Riley, stop." I grab Riley by the arm, but she pushes me away. Alexis snickers when I stumble to the floor.

"Are you okay?" Grace offers me her hand, but I ignore her, crawling back over to Riley. Brooklyn's not moving. The water's up to her shoulders now, and Brooklyn's bent so far over the tub that her knees no longer touch the floor. She doesn't struggle.

"Riley!" I shove my hands into the water, groping for Brooklyn's arm. But the tub is deep. My fingers brush something that feels like hair when Riley grabs me by the shoulders and pulls me back. I hit my elbow on the floor and pain shoots up my arm.

"Calm down," Riley says. "I was just about to let her up."

Riley finally releases Brooklyn's head and leans back on her heels. Her arms are stained brown from the water. Brooklyn stays still. I move closer. Just as I'm about to reach out for her again, Riley grabs Brooklyn by the legs and flips her into the tub. Murky water sloshes onto the marble floor, spraying our feet as Brooklyn's body disappears below the surface. I struggle back onto my knees, but Riley elbows me out of the way before I reach into the bathtub again.

"You're crowding her." Riley narrows her cold eyes as she looks down at me.

"She's *drowning*." I hiss.

"Maybe," Riley says. "If that's God's will." Riley tightens her grip on my arm and starts to pull me out of the bathroom.

"Riley, no!" I try to yank my arm away, but Riley holds on tight. "She's going to die!"

"Lexie, get the door," Riley says.

"No!" I scream. Alexis and Grace follow us out of the bathroom. Even Alexis seems uncertain of Riley's orders, but she still closes the door behind her. I listen for the sound of splashing or screaming—anything to tell me Brooklyn's still alive on the other side of the door. But all I hear is silence.

I pull away from Riley, but she digs her nails into my skin and forces me out of the bedroom and into the hall. While Alexis grabs my arms, Riley slips the tiny key out of her pocket again. There's a silver lock nailed to the doorframe, just like in the basement and at the front door.

Riley planned this—this exact moment. She never meant to baptize Brooklyn. From the beginning, she's been planning to lock her in that bathroom to die.

While Riley is fumbling with the key, I twist my arm away from Alexis, then swing it back, hitting her just below the ribs. Swearing, she doubles over, and I slip out of her grip. I barrel into Riley shoulder first, shoving her aside before she can click the lock shut.

"Sofia, *stop*!" Riley yells. I don't listen. I push the bedroom door open and race for the bathroom. My feet slip over the slick wooden floor, still wet from blood and the dirty tub water.

Riley catches up to me as I reach the bathroom. I try to open the door, but she slaps it shut again.

"You don't know what you're doing," she says, panting. "The devil . . ."

I force the door open, pushing her aside. She slips on a puddle of water near the bathroom door and nearly falls, grabbing hold of the wall to catch herself. The water's surface looks as still as glass. I run to the tub and drop to my knees, thrusting a hand through the brown water. Grace and Alexis crowd behind Riley in the doorway, their footsteps echoing against the marble floors. They hurry over to me, but they're too late. We all are. I stand, pulling my trembling arm out of the water.

"Oh my god," I say, lifting my hands to my mouth.

The bathtub is empty. Brooklyn isn't dead—she's gone.

# CHAPTER FOURTEEN

Brooklyn's gone. I back into Riley and her body stiffens. Her fingers enclose my wrists.

"Where is she?" Riley asks.

"I don't know."

Riley drops my arm. Her eyes widen, and she scans
the bathroom, edging her way toward the door. Every
muscle in her body tenses, as if she expects Brooklyn to
jump out of the walls.

I replay the situation in my head again and again,
like it's a math problem that doesn't add up. I wrap my
arms around my chest and search the bathroom. Grace
clutches the doorframe, her knuckles going white. Alexis

hovers next to her. The corner of her lips twists into something between a smile and a grimace.

"We should have known she would get away," she says. I ignore her and start throwing open the cabinets and closet and shower doors. Empty, all of them. Brooklyn really isn't here.

"Where the *fuck* is she?" Riley slams her open palm against the counter next to the sink.

"Riley—"

"No!" Riley snaps, cutting me off. "We have to find her. Now!"

The weird smile stays painted on Alexis's face. She wraps a long blond strand of hair around one finger. "Don't you get it? She's going to find *us*, and then she's going to kill us."

"No!" Riley jerks her head back and forth. "No. She's too weak. That's not going to happen. Grace, search the basement. The rest of us will look for her on the main floors."

"Why would we look for her inside?" Grace is talking so fast that her words slur together. "She probably went right for the front door, Ri."

"No," Riley insists. "There's no way out, I made sure of it. She's still in the house. We just have to find here."

Grace looks like she might say something else, but instead she presses her lips together and nods.

"You check the bedrooms," Riley says to Alexis. "Sofia and I will look downstairs."

Alexis's smile fades. "You want me to go alone?"

"Just do it." Riley grabs my arm and pulls me from the room into the hall.

Shadows pool in the corners. The plastic hanging from the ceiling rustles in phantom wind. Every second that ticks past pounds at the inside of my skull. I *want* Brooklyn to get away from here. I should be trying to mess Riley up—every moment we waste could be the moment Brooklyn finds an open window or a door without a lock on it.

But as much as I want this to be over and for Brooklyn to be safe, I still don't know what she's capable of. She could be hiding around every corner, waiting on the other side of every wall. She could be anywhere.

A floorboard groans. I jump and spin around, but it's just Grace. She slips down the stairs without a word.

Riley lifts the worn black backpack from the floor where I dropped it. She pulls it open and removes the butcher knife. Her bare feet are practically silent as she moves down the hallway, her back to the wall to keep the floorboards from creaking. I picture the rows of nails wedged into the window frames. There's no way Brooklyn could pull them out of the wood before we reach the first floor. I have to stall Riley.

"Hurry," Riley hisses. She starts down the stairs, and when she reaches the landing, she pauses and cocks her head.

I hear it, too—laughing. At first it's faint, but then it bubbles into a giggle and cuts off abruptly. I turn to look for Alexis, but the hallway behind me is empty. She must've already gone into another room.

"Check on Lexie," Riley says. The top of her head disappears from view as she makes her way to the first floor.

I drag my feet down the hall until I'm standing in front of the window at the end of the hall, next to the cloudy sheet of plastic hanging from the ceiling. Out of the corner of my eye I see something dart across the floor, and I spin around. A knotted rope hangs from the ceiling, casting a shadow that sweeps over the floor as it sways back and forth, back and forth. I reach out to steady it, then tilt my head, following the rope to a door directly above me. The attic.

The plastic sheet rustles, even though there's no wind.

"Brooklyn?" I turn, listening for breathing, but I only hear my own heart hammering in my chest. The blurry shadows between the plastic and the unfinished wall look large enough to be a person. I step closer, my sneakers squeaking against the floor. I lift a shaking hand and wrap my fingers around the plastic.

Someone laughs. I turn so quickly I lose my balance and stumble into the window behind me. The pane shudders, and for a second I'm certain it'll crack. But it holds. The glass feels cold against my bare arms.

There's silence in the empty hallway, then the laughter rises again. It's breathless at first. Then gasping—hysterical. It's coming from the bedroom across from me. I creep forward and push open the door.

Alexis is alone in the empty room, her wide, vacant eyes fixed on some point on the wall in front of her. She balances on the sides of her feet, curling her bare toes inward, like claws. Blood stains the skin along the bottoms of her feet.

Giggling quietly to herself, she twists a long strand of blond hair around her finger. Tighter and tighter she winds it, until her fingertip turns blue.

Then she yanks—pulling the hair right out of her head.

I gasp, covering my mouth with my hands to muffle the sound. Alexis turns her head slowly, like she just realized I was there.

"Don't you think it's funny?" She spreads her fingers and the lock flutters out of her hand, landing on a pile of hair at her feet. Curly strands cover the floor like tiny blond question marks.

"What's funny, Alexis?" I swallow, forcing my eyes away from the hair.

"We're all going to die here," she says in a raspy voice. "We're going to die screaming."

A chill runs down my spine. The door behind me slams open and hits the wall with a crack. I take a deep breath as I turn around, so I don't look as terrified as I feel.

Riley stands in the hallway, one hand curled around the doorframe while the other rests next to her leg, clutching the butcher knife. Brown crusty blood clings to the hems of her jeans. She glances at the hair piled beside Alexis's bare feet but says nothing.

"Find Brooklyn yet?" Alexis asks. Riley taps the knife against her leg.

"She's not downstairs." Riley lowers her hand from the doorframe and steps into the hallway to glance out the window. "Grace thinks—"

A ceiling beam groans above us.

"What was that?" I whisper.

"She's on the roof." Alexis puts a cold hand on my arm. Blond hair clings to her fingertips. "How did she get on the roof?"

The attic door falls open with a crack. Riley jumps and her knife clatters to the floor, its handle sliding beneath the plastic sheet behind her.

I swear under my breath and stumble into Alexis. She releases a string of half-crazy giggles and winds another bunch of blond hair around her finger. The attic door swings back and forth, its hinges creaking.

"No one's there," Riley gasps, relief flooding her face. She kneels, fumbling along the floor with shaking hands. She stares at the dark hole in the ceiling that leads to the attic while she gropes for the knife. I watch the door, too, picturing Brooklyn dropping down on us. Every hair on the back of my neck stands on end.

Out of the corner of my eye, I see a figure appear behind the plastic sheet covering the walls.

Before I can react, Brooklyn tears the sheet from the ceiling and brings it down over Riley's face. Riley screams, and Brooklyn tightens the plastic around her head, pulling her to the floor. She pins Riley's arm to the floor with her shoulder and tightens the plastic around her face.

"Help!" Riley yells, sucking the plastic to her lips. Her fingers find the butcher knife, and she waves it around wildly.

Brooklyn pulls her hand back and slams it into Riley's face. She tries to tear the knife out of her hand, but Riley's gripping it tight as she stabs at the air, blinded from the cloudy plastic covering her face. Gritting her teeth, Brooklyn slams her elbow into Riley's fist. Riley swears, and her fingers go slack around the knife handle. Brooklyn yanks at the knife again, and this time she tugs it free.

"Get away from her!" Alexis races toward them just as Brooklyn struggles to her feet, holding the knife in front of her. Alexis freezes, then takes a step backward.

"Don't you fucking touch me!" Brooklyn shouts. Now that's she's not tumbling around on the ground with Riley, I see just how thrashed she looks. Her clothes are soaked and bloodied, and her hair sticks up in damp spikes. The toilet paper around her destroyed pinkie is gone, revealing the red stub where the tip of her finger used to be. The dirty tub water washed the blood from her skin, but that only makes it easier to see the deep, ugly cuts twisting across her face and legs and arms. Angry purple bruises blossom on her cheeks like flowers.

I lift both arms in surrender and try to catch Brooklyn's eyes. They're shifty and nervous, like a wild animal's. But she holds the knife steady.

"Brooklyn." I take a step toward her and she jabs the knife at me. This is the moment I've been hoping for since Riley first locked us in the basement. The power has shifted. We can finally escape. "Brooklyn, please. I . . ."

Riley pulls the plastic sheet away from her face and pushes herself to her elbow, kicking Brooklyn's legs out from under her. Brooklyn falls backward and slams into the wall. She loses her grip on the knife, and it clatters to the floor. Riley leaps to her feet and rushes her, throwing a shoulder into Brooklyn's gut. Brooklyn regains her footing, and the two girls stumble to the edge of the staircase. Brooklyn starts to fall backward down the stairs and Riley tries to pull away from her, but Brooklyn grabs her by the hair, and they hit the floor together. They teeter at the top of the stairs before rolling over the edge, crashing downward in a tangle of arms and legs.

I race to the top of the staircase, Alexis right behind me. They hit the landing together, and Riley manages to pull herself away from Brooklyn. Brooklyn tries to stand, but Riley kicks her in the chest, sending her plummeting down the rest of the stairs alone. I race after her, but before I reach the landing, Brooklyn rolls onto the floor. She lays there, unmoving.

Riley pushes herself onto her elbow, her breathing ragged. Her hair is slicked back with sweat, and there's a new bruise forming at her jawline. Alexis kneels next to her.

"Does that hurt?" she asks. She tries to touch Riley's bruise, but Riley swats her hand away, glaring at her. I move around them and start down the steps.

Brooklyn's arm is wrenched behind her, her legs curled beneath her body at strange, unnatural angles. The bottom steps are streaked with blood. I hold on to the railing as I make my way to the first floor. Riley says something, but her words blur before they reach my ears. I'm focused entirely on Brooklyn. I watch her eyes, praying for them to flicker open. But they're still.

Halfway down the stairs, I notice Grace hovering next to the wall. It's so dark that her sweatshirt and blue jeans blend into the shadows, and I can't quite make out her expression. She must hear me walking down the stairs because she glances up from Brooklyn's body.

"I think she's dead," Grace says.

# CHAPTER FIFTEEN

"She's not dead." Riley pushes herself to her feet and limps across the landing. "Grace, help me carry her."

Grace stares at Brooklyn's body. Her lower lip trembles. "I . . . I don't . . ."

"We should call the police," I interrupt. "Or an ambulance. She could be . . ." I falter, not wanting to say the word *dead* out loud. "She could be seriously hurt."

Riley winces as she puts weight on her left leg and starts down the stairs, leaning heavily on the banister. She hesitates next to me and lowers her voice so the other girls don't hear.

"What would we tell the police? That the girl we've been torturing accidentally fell down the stairs?"

She says this so bluntly that it takes a moment for her words to sink in. I smell the wine on Riley's breath, but I don't meet her eyes.

"You were here, too, Sofia," Riley continues. "You think *anyone* is going to believe you're innocent just because you tried not hit her when you threw matches on her bare legs?"

"You saw that?" I ask.

"I see everything. Go splash some water on your face. Alexis, Grace, and I will get Brooklyn upstairs."

The thought of using that sludgy brown water on my face makes my stomach churn, but I head up the stairs anyway. I need to be away from Riley.

I pass Alexis on my way up the stairs. She tilts her head to the side, like she's listening to something I can't hear. There's a raw red spot behind her ear where she pulled out her hair.

I creep past her without a word and head for the master bedroom, but when I put a hand on the doorknob, I change my mind. I don't want to go inside the bathroom where Brooklyn almost drowned. Instead, I make my way farther down the hall, opening doors until I find another bathroom. I slip inside and close the door. Then I lock it, turning the knob as quietly as possible so there's no chance Riley will hear it on the first floor.

With a locked door separating me from Riley, I feel safer than I have in hours. I clench my eyes shut and lean my head against the wood, and I have to dig my teeth into my lower lip to keep from sobbing out loud. All the fear and nerves and anxiety bubble up inside me, and I curl my hands into fists. This pulls the mangled skin on my knuckles and makes the torn cuticles around my fingernails sting, reminding me why I'm here in the first place. I lower my hands and take two shaky breaths.

There isn't a mirror hanging on the wall over the sink, just empty white space. It's probably better, I think, as I switch the faucet on and off. I don't want to know what I look like after spending the night in a bloody, smoky basement. I check over my shoulder again and again to make sure the bathtub behind me stays empty. With my back to it, I find myself picturing Brooklyn sitting inside, blood and muddy water streaming from her hair.

It takes a while for water to spurt out of the faucet, and this time it's not muddy and thick, just a little brown. I run the water over my hands, cringing when it hits the skin at my knuckles and around my fingernails.

There's a hair tie next to the faucet, a pink one with a strand of brown hair curled around it. I flick it to the floor, wondering if there's a single room in this house Riley hasn't been. I put my hands back below the water, and, after a moment, it actually feels good. I close my eyes, keeping my hands below the stream until the cold turns them numb.

I turn the faucet off and open my eyes again, glancing back down at the sink just as a cicada pokes its head from the drain. I choke down a scream and stumble back so quickly that my feet bang against the tub and I have to grab hold of the wall to keep myself from falling inside. The cicada crawls out of the drain and into the sink, wings spreading.

Someone bangs on the door. "Sofia! Hurry, we need your help."

Straightening, I unlock the door and pull it open, one eye on the cicada inching across the counter as I slip into the hallway. My skin tingles when I pull the door shut behind me.

"Watch your head," Alexis says, and I duck out of the way as she slides a ladder from the door in the ceiling. Behind her, Grace and Riley drag Brooklyn down the hallway by her arms. I watch her for signs that she's starting to wake, but she doesn't move.

Riley stops at the foot of the ladder. She lets go of Brooklyn's arm, and there's a sick thud as it drops to the floor.

"Sof, you'll have to hold her around her chest and go up backward," Riley says, nodding toward the attic. "Then Grace and I can each take a leg."

"You want to take her to the attic?" I ask. The attic is dark—darker than the basement or the hall next to the kitchen. I doubt there are any windows.

"The basement was getting too smoky," Riley says, wrinkling her nose. "And the attic has a good lock, so there's no chance she'll get away again. Lexie, why don't you run downstairs and get the candles? It'll give us some light."

Obedient as ever, Alexis nods. Her bare feet slap against the floor as she heads down the hallway. Riley takes one of Brooklyn's legs and Grace shuffles forward, doing the same.

"Sof," Riley says, nodding at Brooklyn's chest. "We need your help."

Reluctantly, I slide my arms around Brooklyn's torso and lift her off the ground. My hands tighten around her chest, and I feel the faint *thump thump* of her heartbeat just below her rib cage. Relief floods through me. She's alive.

The three of us slowly make our way up the stairs, stopping every few seconds to redistribute Brooklyn's weight among us. The attic stairs are too steep to go up backward without holding on to anything, so I keep one arm wrapped around Brooklyn's chest and the other hooked over the rickety railing attached to the ladder. Brooklyn isn't heavy, but her body still threatens to slip from my grip.

Finally, we make it into the attic. Raw wooden beams and pink insulation form the walls, and the ceiling angles sharply upward. Stacks of faded *Vogue* magazines sit in the corners, next to Ziploc bags filled with nail polish bottles and an old hair straightener. Empty beer and wine bottles line an entire wall of the attic, arranged by height.

"What is all this?" I ask, panting as we drag Brooklyn off the ladder and onto the unfinished attic floor. Riley glances up and shrugs.

"I come here on my own sometimes," she says. "Just to get away from home."

From the look of things, she comes here all the time. I keep my head ducked until we get Brooklyn to the center of the room, where a thick wooden beam juts up from the floor. Then I lean against another wooden beam, exhausted from my climb up the stairs. The tiny circular window on the far wall looks out over the main street.

I steal a glance out the window, still hoping Josh got my text message and he's on his way now. But the street is empty, and steely black clouds cover the moon, bathing everything in darkness.

"Grace, get me that rope," Riley says, pointing to a metal toolbox next to the wall. Next to the toolbox is the bright yellow nail gun she used to nail the bathroom window shut earlier. I stare down at it, wondering when she brought it up here.

Riley positions Brooklyn against the beam, and when Grace hands her the rope, she begins winding it around Brooklyn's body until there's a thick layer of rope binding

Brooklyn in place. Her head lolls forward, and her chin rests against her chest.

"There," Riley says, knotting the rope behind Brooklyn. "That should hold her."

"We left the backpack downstairs," Grace says. She hovers near the ladder, one hand still gripping the wooden railing. "I'll get it."

Grace climbs down the ladder. Once her head is out of view, Riley turns to me, but before she can say a word, a sharp, clear ringing cuts through the house. The doorbell. Riley's face hardens. My heart jumps in my chest—Josh.

Riley races to the ladder and starts to the second floor, going so fast the rickety wood creaks and groans beneath her weight. I head for the ladder to follow her, but Riley jumps the rest of the way down. She grabs the bottom of the ladder and starts sliding it back into place.

"Watch her," she yells up at me.

"Wait!" I cry out as Riley pushes the ladder up. The door closes, and there's a clicking sound as it locks into place. "Riley!" I shout, banging on the floor. I work the lever to get the ladder to release, but it holds, tight. The doorbell rings again. Heavy footsteps race down the stairs.

*Shit*, I think to myself. She did this on purpose. I push myself to my feet and run across the attic to the window. I press my face up to the glass and squint out onto the street. A bright red pickup is parked by the side of the road. Someone's in the front seat, his arm resting on the open window.

I recognize the rumpled shirt immediately.

"Charlie!" I slam my hand against the window hard, hoping the glass will shatter. "Charlie!" My voice starts to go hoarse, but I don't care—I shout anyway. "Look up! Look up!"

The front door swings open downstairs, and low voices sound just below me. If Charlie hears me at all he doesn't show it. He glances down at the watch on his wrist, then motions impatiently to Josh at the front door. The voices downstairs get louder—it sounds like he and Riley are arguing. I curl my hand into a fist and bang it against the window. The glass shudders, but it doesn't break.

"Sofia?" The voice is weak and raspy. I stop pounding on the glass and turn around. Brooklyn lifts her head and her eyelids flutter open.

"You're awake!" I crouch next to Brooklyn, studying her face. She cringes and tries to move her arm, but the rope holds her tight.

"Fuck," she says, pulling against the rope. "Where am I?"

"Attic." I crawl over to her and try to pull the ropes away with my hands, but they're knotted, tightly, behind her back. "We're locked up here together." Outside, a car engine roars to life.

"No." I stand and turn around to face the window. A flash of white cuts across the street as the truck lights turn on. I press my face to the glass just in time to watch the pickup pull away from the house.

"No!" I slam my fist against the wall. Desperate, frustrated tears sting my eyes. "No!" I shout again. "Come back!"

"Sofia?" Brooklyn shifts on the floor, making the rope binding her groan. Too numb to answer her, I slide to the ground, choking back tears.

"Josh and Charlie were here," I explain. "But they're gone now."

Brooklyn turns her head to the side. Her eyes sweep across the room, studying the old bottles and dog-eared magazines. She wrinkles her nose. "And Riley and the others? Where are they?"

"Downstairs."

Brooklyn's eyes widen. "So we're alone?"

I nod toward the door behind her. "Yeah, but we're locked in."

"Attic doors like that lock automatically, but there's a trick to get them to release." Brooklyn motions to the ropes with her chin. "Untie me and I'll show you."

I study Riley's old things as I cross the attic toward Brooklyn. Riley's porcelain doll sits next to an ancient pink plastic CD player. A new crack cuts between the doll's eyes, like a scar. I shiver, thoroughly creeped out.

I crouch next to Brooklyn and start working on the knots binding her to the pillar. Behind me, something clicks.

"*Shout to the . . . Shout to the . . . Shout to the . . .*" The words fill each nook and cranny of the attic, echoing off the exposed beams.

I stand and stumble backward. "What the hell is that?"

"It's that CD player." Brooklyn says, studying something behind me. "You must have kicked it."

"*Shout . . . shout . . . shout—*"

I turn and grab the CD player, hitting the power button. As soon as the music cuts off I hear something else—scratching. It's coming from the corner.

"Do you hear that?" I ask, moving toward the noise. It goes silent.

"It's probably just rats," Brooklyn says, shifting on the floor. "Sof, come on, you have to untie me."

"Right." I shake my head and hurry back over to Brooklyn. "Downstairs," I say as I pull at her ropes. "In the basement, you said you pushed that teacher off a ladder."

"*Lies,*" Brooklyn insists. "Everything I 'confessed' was a lie. I thought Riley would let me go if I played her game."

"I knew it," I say, and a wave of relief washes over me. I work my fingers around the knot, but I can't manage to pull it free. Frustrated, I sit back on my heels.

"I need scissors or a knife or . . ." I spot the toolbox under the window and get an idea. I race over to it, and dig around inside for one of the long, slightly crooked nails. "This might work."

I crouch next to Brooklyn again and try to work the nail through the knot. I manage to loosen it a little before the sweaty nail slips from my fingers. I swear under my breath and fumble along the floor with my fingers.

The scratching sounds in the corner. They're louder this time. Brooklyn tenses beneath her ropes.

"Pretty big rat," she whispers. The shuffling cuts off, and the attic goes silent.

I find the nail and stand, inching toward the noise. It came from the far corner of the attic, directly above the empty room where Alexis pulled out her own hair. The floor over there is bare, empty. It's kind of strange— Riley's magazines and cosmetics pack every corner of the attic. Except that one.

I kneel on the floor next to the wall.

"Is something there?" Brooklyn hisses. I hold a finger to my lips, quieting her. There is something, but it's quiet enough that I couldn't hear it across the room. The noise sounds familiar now. It's a low, rasping sound that I can't quite place.

I lean into the wall and press my ear against the wood. I recognize the noise now.

Breathing.

I yank my face away from the wall and dart back, an animalistic survival instinct kicking in. My entire body tenses to run.

Then my brain catches up. Someone's hiding back there, watching us. I narrow my eyes, and I lift a hand to the wall. It's too dark up here to see, but I feel a shift in the wood. A door.

"Sofia, what the hell?" Brooklyn hisses. I wedge the crooked nail into the narrow opening. The door creaks open, revealing a shadowy, cramped crawl space. Two eyes blink in the darkness. I startle as Grace moves into the dim attic light, her skin ashen. Sweat gathers beneath her hairline.

"Grace, you scared me half to death!" I say.

"Riley made me," she whispers before I get the chance to ask her what she's doing. "She wanted to see what you would do when you were alone."

My throat goes dry. "Why?" I ask. The sound of the attic door falling open interrupts us, and Riley appears at the top of the ladder. She glances at Brooklyn's ropes and the crooked nail in my hands.

"Why do you think?" Riley says.

# CHAPTER SIXTEEN

I back away from Grace's crawl space, dropping the nail. It hits the floor with a soft ping, then rolls to a stop next to Brooklyn's knee. Riley follows it with her eyes.

"What were you doing, Sofia?" she asks. Grace crawls out of her hiding space and inches along the back wall to the alcove by the door.

Brooklyn collapses against the beam, and her face slackens. The hope drains out of it, leaving her cheeks sunken. Her hair forms stiff blond spikes that stick out from her head like thorns.

"Just let me go," she whispers, digging her fingernails into the wooden floor. "Please."

Riley ignores her pleading. "You were going to untie her," she says to me, taking a step closer. Brooklyn gasps, releasing jagged bursts of air that make her chest heave. A tear crawls down her cheek.

The dark of the attic paints Riley's face black and gray. Her cheeks and eyes look hollow, her skin ashen. I step away from her, but the wall with the window is directly behind me. I press my hands flat against the cold glass. Outside, the wind howls.

"Riley, I . . ."

"You were going to let her go!" Riley slaps me across the face. I gasp, and pain spreads through my cheeks. Grace cringes, staring at the floor. She won't meet my eyes.

"What did you think would happen?" Riley continues. "That you and Brooklyn would race downstairs and run off with your boyfriends?"

"Please," Brooklyn begs, and in that second I hate her. *I* want to cry and beg and fall apart. But instead I stare into Riley's icy, empty eyes and try to be strong. Brooklyn inhales and mouths the word without making a sound. *Please.*

Riley slaps me again. I cringe against the sting of her hand.

"Do you think I didn't know you texted them? That I didn't hear you fumbling with the phone in the basement? I know everything, Sofia!"

*How?* I want to ask. *How do you see everything, know everything?* I wonder briefly if she installed security cameras when she nailed all the windows shut, but even that doesn't explain how she seems to see inside my head, how she knows what I'm thinking and feeling.

"Riley," I gasp, lifting a hand to my cheek. "I'm . . ."

"Shut up! Don't you see? God wanted this to happen. He wanted you to fail so you'd understand that the only way out of this house is through *him.*"

Riley's face crumples and she sinks to her knees. "I knew this would happen," she says, her hands trembling as she lifts them to her face. "I tried so hard to keep us all strong, but I knew, I *knew* one of us would fall! Now it's up to me to bring you back. "

I watch Riley for a long moment before I realize she's crying. Brooklyn stares at Riley's shaking shoulders, her eyes reflecting the same anger I felt moments ago. Riley doesn't deserve to cry. She hasn't earned it.

A warm yellow glow appears at the door in the floor. The ladder creaks, and the glow comes closer. Riley straightens and wipes her eyes. Alexis appears at the ladder holding a thick white candle.

"Where's the knife?" Riley asks, her voice steady. The skin around her eyes is slightly red, but otherwise there's no sign she was crying.

"Downstairs, in the backpack." Alexis puts the candle

on the floor to the left of the ladder and starts to climb into the attic. The flickering light fills the room with shadows.

"Go get it," Riley snaps, pushing herself back to her feet. She starts to pace, and her stiff, bloodstained jeans sound scratchy, like dried paper dragging across the floor. She shoots a look at Grace. "Both of you. I need a moment alone with Sofia."

"Don't go," I say. As soon as the words leave my mouth, I know I've made a mistake. Riley stops pacing and levels a glare on me that could burn through skin.

"What's going on?" Alexis asks, hovering near the ladder. She shifts her gaze from me to Riley to Grace.

"Please," I say, but I'm watching Riley now. I realize Riley could never feel pain. Riley doesn't feel anything.

"Get the knife," Riley says again. Alexis frowns but heads back down the ladder anyway. Grace shuffles after her. I don't realize I'm reaching for them until they're already gone. My hand hovers in the air, grasping at nothing.

"You're letting the devil manipulate you." Riley turns away from me, talking to herself now. "That's why you texted Josh, why you were going to let Brooklyn go. That's the only explanation."

"Riley . . ." I start, but she cuts me off.

"The devil feeds on your weakness, Sofia! Don't you

see how Brooklyn's working you? How she's using you? This is what the devil does!"

Riley's voice rises to a hysterical scream. It bounces off the walls of the attic. She stops walking and lifts her hands to her head, running her fingers through her hair. The hair comes loose from her ponytail and frizzes around her face.

"Riley," I say, edging toward the ladder. I try to make my voice as soothing as possible. "Riley, I'm not possessed. You have to calm down."

"Calm down?" Riley stumbles over Brooklyn's leg to dart in front of me, blocking my path to the door. Brooklyn doesn't even flinch but watches us with wide, curious eyes. "How am I supposed to calm down, Sofia? We tried everything. Everything! None of it has worked. And you were just going to let her go."

The ladder creaks, and Alexis climbs into the attic again, Grace behind her. She's carrying a box of granola bars, the black backpack looped over one shoulder.

"Give me that." Riley yanks the backpack from Grace's arm and rips it open violently. The silver zipper pops off and clatters to the floor. Grace backs away from Riley, rubbing her shoulder. Riley pulls the butcher knife out and lets the bag drop. Hand shaking, she holds the knife in front of her. The blade trembles in her grip.

"Sofia betrayed us." Her eyes meet mine, and cold

dread creeps up over my bones. She takes a step closer, gesturing with the knife while she speaks. "She tried to let Brooklyn go."

"Riley, wait." I raise my hands in front of my chest, stumbling back against the wall. I can't tear my eyes away from the knife. It looks different somehow, like it's watching me. It's the same knife Riley used to cut off Brooklyn's finger, the one that sliced open her skin and spilled her blood onto the floor. It has a taste for blood now.

"What are you doing?" Grace whispers. Riley pushes the point of the blade to my chest. I picture her thrusting it into my body, and my head spins. I place a hand flat against the wall behind me to steady myself.

"I don't know. What do we do to sinners?"

The knife winks at me, or maybe it's just the light reflecting off its blade. I squeeze my eyes shut. I'm just scared, imagining things. But then I open my eyes and Brooklyn is staring me, her eyes glowing red. She runs her tongue over her lips, smearing blood across her mouth. Her voice echoes in my head: *Now you're reborn.*

I blink and Brooklyn's eyes are normal again; there's no blood on her mouth. Her lower lip trembles as she watches me.

Riley lowers the knife from my chest and places it just below my wrist. "In the Old Testament, when God's people sinned, they'd cut off the part of their body that failed him," she says. "This is the hand that failed your God. Would you sacrifice it, if it's what the Lord commanded?"

The blade pricks my skin. Brooklyn clenches her hand into a fist, but all I see is the bloody stub where her finger should be. Fear bubbles inside me.

"Riley, no. *Please.*" I squeeze my eyes shut, and tears leak onto my cheeks. I remember Brooklyn screaming in the basement and the sick sound of flesh dropping to the floor. I try to breathe, but it's as if someone's hands are wrapped around my lungs, squeezing them. I struggle to inhale, and my tears quickly become ugly sobs. "Don't, please, don't."

Suddenly the cold blade is no longer pressed against my wrist. Something clatters to the floor, and then Riley's arms are around my neck, pulling me close to her. She rubs her hand in circles on my back.

"Shh, Sofia, it's okay," she whispers, hugging me tight. "It's okay, I won't hurt you."

I wrap my arms around Riley without thinking and lower my head to her shoulder. Relief spreads through my body like a salve, calming the hysteria in my head, erasing the crazy things I thought I saw. Riley moves her hand to the back of my head and pats down my hair.

"You have to fight the power of Satan," she begs. "I need you with me on this. We can still help her, Sofia."

"How?" I say into her neck. I pull away from her and wipe the tears from my cheek with the back of my hand.

For a moment no one says a word. I look from Riley to Grace to Alexis, but their faces are all blank.

"You didn't humble yourselves," Brooklyn's voice cuts through the silence. Riley turns, and Brooklyn smiles at her wickedly. I picture her glowing red eyes, her mouth dark with blood, but force the image away. That wasn't real, just a trick my fear played on me.

Alexis takes a step away from the ladder. "What are you talking about?" she asks.

"Your sins," Brooklyn says. She leans forward, pulling at the ropes binding her to the beam. "None of you told the truth about your sins, did you?"

# CHAPTER SEVENTEEN

"No one lied," Riley says, too quickly. Heat climbs over my face, and I shift my eyes to the floor. *I lied,* but I can't admit that now. Riley nearly cut off my hand for trying to untie Brooklyn. I can't imagine what she'd cut off if she found out I lied to God.

"Guys, *tell* her," Riley hisses. Alexis stares at her feet to keep from meeting our eyes. Grace backs up all the way to the wall, pulling her sweatshirt sleeves down over her wrists.

"They're not the only ones who lied, Riley." Brooklyn's face stays blank, but her voice seems almost amused.

Riley's face hardens. "*I* didn't lie," she insists.

"You didn't tell the whole truth, though," Alexis says. She clenches her hands in front of her, and the tips of her hair brush against her fingers. "None of us told the whole truth."

"Does that mean you want to start?" Brooklyn asks. Alexis winds a strand of hair around one finger, saying nothing. "How about you, Riley?"

"Shut up," Riley says, staring down at her knife on the ground. But she doesn't move toward it or threaten Brooklyn. "I told the truth," she insists again.

"What about Grace?" Brooklyn searches the shadows in the corner for Grace. "Did you admit the whole truth about your little addiction?"

Grace's eyes shift first to Alexis, then to Riley, and finally to me. She hunches up her shoulders, nearly disappearing into her oversize sweatshirt. "I told you I had a problem with drugs and I did," she says.

"Ritalin," Brooklyn corrects her. "Is that all you've ever tried?"

"No." Grace's voice breaks. She picks up the backpack off the floor where Riley dropped it and pulls out a bottle of wine. She yanks out the cork and swigs it back.

"What else have you tried?" Alexis asks. Grace takes another drink of wine.

"It was only Ritalin at first," Grace admits. "I was only going to take a few to study, just like I said. But the high felt so good. It was like my brain went still, like everything fell away except for the thing I was doing. Everything just got so . . . easy."

Grace pauses for a beat and shifts her eyes back down. Brooklyn taps her combat boot against the floor.

"Well?" Brooklyn says. "Don't stop now. You were just getting to the good part."

Grace weaves her hands around the wine bottle nervously. Her electric-blue nails stand out against the dark glass. I stare at them, remembering when I first met Grace, when she seemed impossibly exotic and cool. Now she's vulnerable, naked.

"You don't have to tell us this, Grace," I say.

"We all have to come clean before God," Riley murmurs. She stares blankly at the wall ahead of her. "She does have to tell."

"You all do." Brooklyn looks at me when she says this, and now I'm sure I hear amusement in her voice. Her eyes seem to peel away my skin and see directly into my brain, to the things I'm most ashamed of. I turn back to the wine bottle, focusing my attention on Grace's chipped blue nails again.

"I should've stuck with Ritalin," Grace says, almost to herself. "But I found Xanax in my mom's bathroom one morning. That was even better. After that, I tried my dad's Ambien and some X from a girl at school."

"Grace, the Lord forgives you," Riley says in a hushed voice. She takes the bottle of wine from Grace's hands and drinks. "We all fall. All of us."

Grace smiles through her tears. The candlelight flickers, reflecting the lines they made down her face. From behind her, Brooklyn starts to cackle.

"Are you kidding me?" she says. She leans her head against the pillar, laughing harder. "You're *still* lying!"

"Grace, just tell her. Let's get this over with," Alexis says. Grace grabs the bottle back from Riley and raises it to her lips. This time, she drinks deeply. A red drip oozes out from the side of her mouth and dribbles down over her chin.

Gasping for breath as she lowers the bottle, Grace continues. "When my brother broke his leg this summer, he left his Oxy pills in the bathroom like they were *nothing*. I had to stare at them every morning while I was brushing my teeth." Grace hiccups and takes another drink of wine. "What would you have done?"

Alexis takes the wine bottle out of Grace's hands. "It's okay," she starts, but Grace shakes her head.

"It's not okay!" she yells. Tears fall down her cheeks, faster and faster. She hiccups again. "I want to be cured. I want to be better. But . . . but I . . ." She can't talk now—she's crying too hard. She lowers her face to her hands, sinking to her knees. "I want to be better," she sobs.

Alexis crouches next to Grace, wrapping her arms around her shoulders. "It's okay," she murmurs into her ear. Even Riley crosses the attic to kneel next to her. She closes her eyes, and her lips move in a silent prayer.

I move toward Grace, but Brooklyn lifts her head before I can crouch next to her. Her eyes widen, and she leans her head toward Grace. She's trying to tell me something.

All at once, it clicks. Grace is an addict—addicts have drugs.

No wonder Brooklyn was egging Grace on. Drugs mean freedom—escape. If Grace has pills with her, I can find them and put them in the wine they've all been drinking. If I add enough, they'll pass out.

Riley whispers "Amen," and her eyes flicker open. She picks up the wine and takes a deep drink, staring at me over the top of the bottle.

I twist my face into what I hope is a sympathetic expression and stoop beside her, looping one arm over her shoulder and the other over Grace's.

"Amen," I whisper.

# CHAPTER EIGHTEEN

"Who's next?" Brooklyn asks. She's trying to distract them. If they keep admitting their sins, they won't pay attention to me. And I'll have enough time to find Grace's pills.

"How do you know all this?" Grace wipes her tears away with her palm as she turns to Brooklyn. Alexis pulls away from her, pushing her hair back behind one ear.

Brooklyn smirks. A wild thought flies through my head—maybe she reads minds. Maybe Brooklyn already knows everything we've done.

"Grace stares at the floor when she lies," Riley says before Brooklyn can answer. "Anyone can see that."

Grace blushes and pushes herself to her feet. She backs into an alcove just off the main area in the attic and presses her body against the wall, like she's trying to disappear into the wood.

Brooklyn's eyes linger on her. "It's almost worth the fire, the drowning, and the brutal torture to hear about how shitty you all are," she says.

"Do we need to gag you again?" Riley motions to the duct tape on the floor, but she leans over to pick up the wine bottle instead.

"What's the matter, Riley?" Brooklyn groans, struggling to move beneath the layers of rope binding her in place. "Afraid what your friends will think when you *really* admit your sins?"

"I already admitted them," Riley insists. She pushes a sweaty lock of hair off her forehead with the back of her hand, then drinks deeply from the wine bottle.

I scan the attic while Riley drinks, wondering where Grace stowed her pills. But Brooklyn's words stay with me. *Afraid what your friends will think when you* really *admit your sins?*

I push the question away, and my eyes fall on the black backpack sitting by the stairs. Grace was the one who brought the bag up here. It would've been easy for her to slip a bottle inside.

"Or maybe you should go next, Lexie." Brooklyn

shifts her eyes to Alexis. "You could tell everyone why your sister's really in a coma."

"You don't know what you're talking about," Alexis hisses.

"I know more than you think." Brooklyn's wolf grin deepens.

Riley lowers the wine bottle. "What's she talking about?"

Alexis leans back on her heels and grabs a lock of hair, winding it roughly around her finger. I think of the way she looked standing in that empty room with wispy locks of white-blond curls piled at her feet, like a fairy-tale princess stuck in a horror story.

"She's just making things up," Alexis says. The skin around her fingernail starts to turn blue, but still she winds the hair tighter.

I edge my way closer to the staircase and the back-pack. Nerves pull at my skin like tiny, pinching fingers and my heart jackhammers in my chest. I move slowly toward Grace, inching my feet across the floorboards. She hums a pop song under her breath, her eyes fixated on her shoes.

"You said you hoped she'd never wake up." Brooklyn allows each word to hang in the air for a beat before she continues. "That's not the first time you wanted her dead, is it?"

Alexis shakes her head. "I never wanted that!" There's a faint sound, almost a rip, and the hair drifts away from her fingers. Alexis pushes herself clumsily to her feet, nearly stumbling into me as I inch along the wall behind her. Before she reaches for another lock of hair, Riley takes her hand.

"Just tell us what happened, Lex." Still holding Alexis's hand, she drinks from the wine bottle again. Her words slur a little when she says, "We all have to admit our sins before God."

Grace hums louder. The song tugs at my memory, just out of reach. She takes a step toward the stairs and lifts the faded black backpack from the floor, hugging it to her chest like a teddy bear. I drive my teeth into my lower lip. *Damnit!*

"Are you nervous?" Grace asks me. I'm so distracted by the backpack I almost don't hear her.

"What?"

"About telling your sin." Grace hums another line from the song, and now I remember where I heard it before. It was at that party I went to, the one at the house by the train tracks, where the jocks rated every girl who walked through the front door. Karen invited me to that party.

"No," I say, but I *am* nervous. Not because I don't want to tell my sin, but because I don't want to relive it.

Grace starts humming again, and now it's too late. I'm there, at the party. The entire house trembles as a train rolls past. . . .

*I nervously make my way through the crowd of kids inside, stopping in the kitchen to get a soda. When I turn around, Lila's behind me. Her black hair hangs down over her narrow shoulders in a perfect, glossy sheet. Her red-painted lips curl up in a cruel smile.*

*"Wait." Lila frowns, and her eyes shift to my hair. "You have something caught in your hair."*

*Lila reaches forward and plucks something from my hair. The curl of her lips hardens as she pulls her hand away.*

*She's holding a Q-tip.*

*Some of the kids behind her start to snicker, but Lila manages to keep a straight face as she asks, "Now, where did this come from, Greasy?"*

*More laughter. It bubbles up around me until I can't tell who it's coming from anymore. Cheeks burning, I push past Lila.*

*Everybody at the party is staring at me, laughing behind their hands and into their beer cups. I try to move forward, but the kids in front of me crowd together, blocking my path.*

*"Where are you going, Greasy?" a girl with frizzy red hair asks. She tosses a Q-tip at me, and it gets caught on my sweater.*

*Another Q-tip soars across the room and hits me in the cheek. A third flies past my arm. Before I know it, everyone's throwing Q-tips and laughing. Horrified, I cover my face with my hands, but still they catch in my hair and on my clothes. I finally find a break in the crowd and force my way through the people—and run right into Karen.*

*She's standing next to Erin, holding a beer.*

*"Come on, Sofia," she says, breaking out into a grin. "Take a joke."*

*I stare, dumbfounded, as she lifts her hand and tosses a Q-tip right at me. It bounces off my chest and drops to the floor.*

"Sofia, are you okay?" Grace loosens her hold on the backpack. I could take it from her now, but instead I lean against the wall. Sweat forms on the back of my neck.

With my eyes closed I smell the stale beer that coated the floors in that house, I hear the cruel laughter and the distant roar of the train. After that night I promised myself I'd never go to another party, never again be friends with girls who laughed at other people's pain. Now I'm trapped in an attic, and the only way I'm getting out is by reliving the worst night of my life.

"I'm fine," I say, easing my eyes back open. Grace nods sympathetically, but I don't meet her eyes—I'm staring at the backpack. I was wrong; there is another way out of here. I just have to find those pills.

Alexis's voice rises into a yell. "It's not like Brooklyn's

saying it was!" Alexis looks from Brooklyn to Riley, and her lower lip begins to tremble. "Riley, you know how Carly is," she pleads.

Riley swirls the wine in the bottle, watching liquid slosh up against the sides of the glass. "I know you guys are really competitive."

"Exactly," Alexis says. "But it's not even a competition, because Carly *always* wins. Carly got into Stanford, and Carly's boyfriend is perfect. Do you have any idea what it's like hearing about how wonderful she is all the time?"

Alexis sobs and lowers her head to her hands. Her hair sweeps over her face like a curtain.

"Come on, Alexis," Riley says. She takes another swig from the bottle, then wipes the wine off her top lip with the back of her hand. "Finish the story. Tell us what happened next."

Sniffling, Alexis pushes the hair from her face. "It was an accident, like I said. Carly has a really bad peanut allergy. She has to carry an EpiPen wherever she goes. Last year she and my mom went on a juice cleanse to get ready for the annual charity gala my mom runs, and the only things they could eat were these gross smoothies made from spinach and lemon juice. One day I just . . . I snuck a peanut into Carly's smoothie. Just one."

Alexis's admission shocks me so much that I

forget about the night of the party and Grace's pills—everything but what she just said.

"You poisoned your sister on purpose?" I ask. I think about what my grandmother always said about confession as Alexis studies our faces, looking for sympathy.

*"Words, they have power,* mija. *When you say your sin out loud, you admit it to yourself as well as to God."*

If I were Alexis, I'd have taken that secret to the grave, no matter what Riley or Brooklyn said.

"She was supposed to have her EpiPen with her!" Alexis continues. "Once she took her shot she'd have been fine. My parents would have made her stay home to rest like they always did when she had a reaction. I could have gone to the gala in her place. But she didn't take her EpiPen that day, because it didn't fit into the stupid designer bag she wanted to carry. So instead of getting sick, she . . ."

"She went into a coma," Grace says.

Alexis grabs for another strand of her hair, but Riley slaps her hand away. "You're sick," she says.

"Stop it!" Alexis yells. "You're drunk!"

"Don't you dare turn this around on me." Riley's eyes are red-rimmed, but I can't tell if it's from the wine or the shock of what Alexis just admitted.

"Why not?" Alexis's voice trembles. "I'm not the only one who's sinned."

Riley slaps her. Alexis's head snaps to the side, and her hands fly to her face. When she turns back to Riley, her mouth hangs open in shock.

"I don't have anything to hide," Riley says. "Whatever I am, whatever I've done, it's *nothing* compared with trying to kill your own flesh and blood."

"You're lying." Alexis sways back and forth, her weight on the balls of her feet, like a ballerina's. There's a light in her eyes that I don't quite understand. It's manic, unhinged. "You're lying, but I know the truth. I know *everything* you've done."

# CHAPTER NINETEEN

I pull my arms close to my chest, staring through the open attic door to the ladder descending to the shadowy hallway below. I imagine prying the nails out of a windowsill with my bare hands. My fingertips sting just thinking about it, but I shift toward the door anyway.

"You pretend you're so much better than the rest of us," Alexis shouts. "But you're a *slut*. Every word out of your mouth is a lie."

"Like anyone would believe you after what you've done," Riley spits out.

Grace hiccups again. She's crouched in the alcove next to the door, hugging the backpack. The attic is small—maybe only ten feet long and five feet wide—but because of the angle of the ceiling and walls I can't see what she's doing. Still, she's the only one between me and the door. She'd catch me before I made it to the stairs.

"I'd believe her," Brooklyn says. A strand of hair falls over her eyes. She blows at it, and it flutters back over her forehead. "Whatever happened to coming clean before the Lord, Riley?"

Alexis laughs and shakes her head so violently her neck cracks. "Why are we even here? Because Brooklyn screwed around with your *boyfriend*, right?"

"Shut up." Riley's voice trembles.

"But that's not really true, is it?" Alexis says. "Because he's not your boyfriend. Not anymore. He dumped you two weeks ago."

"I told you to shut up!" Riley screams. Her hands fly to her head, covering her ears.

"And you know what the best part is?" Alexis yells back. "He dumped you because you're a *slut*. He found out what you did with Tom. Why don't you tell that to your precious God, Riley?"

Riley squeezes her eyes shut, shaking her head. I hadn't been paying attention, but now I turn toward Riley.

"Tom?" I repeat. "Wait, Josh's brother Tom? The one Grace . . ."

Grace steps out of the alcove. "What did you do with him?" she asks, her voice cracking.

Riley's red-rimmed eyes widen. "Grace, I . . ."

Grace drops the backpack and steps forward, grabbing Riley's arm. "I've had a crush on Tom since I moved here!" she says, but I'm no longer listening. All I see is the backpack abandoned in the alcove.

"I know," Riley says. "But . . ."

"Did you sleep with him?" Grace interrupts. Riley hesitates, and Grace yells, "Tell the truth!"

"It was just one time. It didn't mean anything!" Riley says. She turns back to Alexis. "You bitch. That was a secret."

"Isn't that the point?" Alexis hisses. "We're all sharing our secrets. You don't get to judge me if you're not willing to own up to yours."

Riley shouts something back at Alexis and their voices grow louder, until they're both screaming at each other and I can't make out what they're actually saying. Brooklyn kicks my ankle lightly with her combat boot, and I look over at her. *Pills*, she mouths, nodding at the backpack.

Grace buries her face in her hands. I creep behind her, sliding into the alcove, where I'm hidden from everyone but Brooklyn. Star-shaped Christmas lights hang from the ceiling above me, and Riley pinned three dead butterflies into the wood with tiny pink pushpins. Their tissue-thin wings look brittle enough to break.

My sneaker brushes up against the bag and I crouch down, pulling it onto my lap. Grace lifts the bottle of wine to her lips again and again, trying to drown all the things she just heard with booze. As long as she doesn't turn around, I'm safe.

I unzip the backpack and thrust my hand inside, digging for the pill bottle. Riley's and Alexis's shadows stretch over the floor. If either of them takes a single step to the left they'll see right into the alcove. My fingers bump up against the wooden cross, but that's it—there's nothing else inside the backpack. Frustrated, I rip open the front pocket.

"I came here to help you, you ungrateful bitch!" Alexis yells. "But now I don't know why I bothered. You obviously don't care about anyone but yourself."

Alexis's footsteps pound against the floor. I glance up as she steps directly in front of the alcove. *Shit.* I drop the backpack and stand, but her back is to me. I don't think she saw anything.

"Alexis, don't," Riley says. Over Grace's shoulder I watch Riley grab Alexis's arm, dragging her back to the center of the room. My heart thuds against my chest. Grace takes another swig of wine, watching the fight unfold like it is a movie.

"You leave when I tell you to leave," Riley says. Her fingers grip Alexis's arm so tightly her skin starts to turn red.

Alexis tries to yank her arm away. "Let go," she says. But Riley holds on tight.

Heart hammering against my chest, I kneel and pull the backpack to my side. I grope against the fabric inside until my fingers enclose a plastic cylinder. I pull it out and quickly turn it in my hand to see the label.

AMBIEN, it reads. My heart thuds against my rib cage. This is it. This is finally *it*.

A floorboard creaks. A chill streaks down my spine, and I look up. Grace's dark eyes are turned toward me, watching me.

Time freezes. My mind moves at hyper-speed, trying to come up with some excuse, some reason to be digging through the bag for the pills. But I can't think of a single reason, and all I can do is wait for Grace to call out to the others and tell them what I'm doing.

Grace considers me for a moment. Then she lifts a finger to her mouth, shooting a look over her shoulder at Riley and Alexis. Neither has noticed us. Yet.

Satisfied they aren't watching, Grace sets the wine bottle on the floor next to me, then turns back around, as if she didn't see me with the pills at all.

# CHAPTER TWENTY

I ease the bottle open and pour the pills into my hand. Ten white pills tumble onto my palm. I don't know anything about drugs, but ten seems like a lot—definitely enough to take out a teenage girl. I pry open one of the capsules and dump the fine white powder into the wine bottle.

Riley's jeans scratch against the floor as she paces around the room. Grace is angled in front of me to keep Riley from seeing what I'm doing, but I still freeze, certain I'm about to be discovered. The powder from the pills sticks to my fingers and the mouth of the bottle. I swear under my breath and try to brush it all into the wine.

"I thought you two were so close," Brooklyn says, her voice dripping with fake sympathy. If either Alexis or Riley notices she's making fun of them, they don't show it. They only seem to see each other.

"You were always a shitty friend," Alexis yells, her voice cracking. She wraps a long blond strand of hair around one finger and gives it a sudden, violent tug. "The only reason we even hang out is because you can't stand to be alone."

"I think you have that backward, Lexie." Riley's voice is quiet and even, barely above a whisper. Alexis stands in the middle of the attic while Riley moves around her, an animal circling her prey. "The only reason we're friends is because you need someone to obsess over. You've been pretending to be me since you were eight years old. I just can't get rid of you."

The quieter Riley speaks, the more outraged Alexis grows. "Why not? Because *God* wouldn't want you to?" Alexis shouts. "You hide behind God so no one will see how screwed up you really are."

"I'm not ashamed of anything I've done," Riley continues, rounding back on Alexis. "But you have everything to be ashamed of. You tried to kill your sister! How can any of us ever trust you again?"

Alexis's breathing gets heavier, and she starts to cry. Grace stiffens in front of me. Alexis must've pulled another clump of hair out of her head, but I refuse to look up and watch her. My fingers feel thick and clumsy as I work them around the pills.

"You're wrong," Alexis says.

"Am I?" Riley's voice takes on a cruel, almost gleeful edge. I recognize that tone by now—it means she knows something the rest of us don't.

"If I'm so wrong, why are you still hiding?" Riley continues. "You're keeping secrets from all of us."

The floorboards creak as Alexis takes a step back.

"Stop it," she says. I have the final pill pinned between two fingers, but I peer around the corner to see what's happening.

Riley has Alexis backed against the wall. I can't see Riley's face, but Alexis looks broken. Her eyes are red-rimmed, and she releases a choked, gasping sob. She shakes her head and covers her hair with her hands.

"No," she whispers. "Riley, *please*."

Riley slaps Alexis's hands away and pulls her forward by the head, brushing her long, beautiful hair back with one hand. Beneath the top layer of perfect blond locks, Alexis's entire scalp is red and raw, spotted with still-bleeding scabs.

Alexis pulls away from Riley and tries, desperately, to smooth her hair back in place. Her face crumples, and she drops to her knees, her shoulders shaking with silent sobs. She lifts her hand to the hair just behind her left ear and starts compulsively winding a lock around her finger—tighter and tighter—until it comes off in her hands. Blood spots the skin at her scalp.

"You're disgusting. Soon you won't have any hair left."

Brooklyn releases a slightly hysterical-sounding laugh at the exact second the pill hits the floor. Frowning, Riley pivots to face her.

"What's so funny?" she hisses.

"Hurry," Grace mutters under her breath. I refocus my attention on the pills. I wedge my thumbnail into the last capsule and pull it apart. The white powder dissolves into the wine.

"Your little catfight is just adorable," Brooklyn says. "Which of your friends are you going to turn on next?"

"Shut up," Riley spits out. She crosses the attic and kicks Brooklyn in the shin. Brooklyn makes a big show of squeezing her eyes shut and yelling out in pain, but I know she said those things for me, to distract Riley from what I'm doing.

Grabbing the wine bottle, I stand and slip out of the alcove, placing a hand on Riley's shoulder.

"She's messing with you," I say, squeezing Riley's arm. I lift the wine bottle to my mouth and tip it back, but I keep my lips tight to keep from drinking the drugged wine. I pretend to swallow as I lower the bottle. "She wants you and Alexis to tear each other apart."

"Give me that." Riley's face is blank as she rips the bottle from my hands. She stares down at it for a long moment. Across from us, Alexis sinks to the floor. She sobs quietly, her hands curled into fists around her hair.

"You're right." Riley smiles as she turns the wine bottle in her hand, watching the liquid slosh up against the sides. "We have to trust each other."

"Exactly," I say. "We can't let Brooklyn come between us."

Riley's smile immediately disappears. "We can't let *Brooklyn* come between us," she repeats. She lingers on Brooklyn's name and tightens her grip around the bottle.

Grace weaves her fingers together. She glances at me nervously, but I won't look at her. I can't tear my eyes away from Riley.

Riley shifts her eyes back up to me. They're the eyes of a predator: dead and calculating.

"Didn't realize you were a big drinker," she says, lifting the bottle.

"What?" I swallow, waiting, but Riley holds the wine just below her mouth. The glass brushes against her lower lip.

"The wine," she says. "You seem more interested in it all of the sudden."

"I guess I'm just thirsty," I say.

Riley inhales the scent of the wine, closing her eyes. "Me, too," she murmurs. She tips the bottle back and the wine slides forward. I hold my breath, but the second seems to stretch for an eternity. Sweat breaks out along my palms.

Just before she drinks, Riley's eyes flicker back open.

"Do you think I'm stupid?" she whispers. My throat goes dry.

"Of course not."

Riley lowers the bottle. "What did you put in here?"

Dread creeps into my gut. "I . . ."

Riley heaves the wine bottle across the room. It shatters against the wall just a few feet from where Alexis is crouched, spraying the floor with glass. Alexis flinches, throwing her hands over her face. The thick liquid oozes down the boards behind her head, but the wood drinks the wine before it slides to the floor, leaving behind a deep red stain.

"You tell me you want me to trust you, but you're lying to me!" Riley screams.

"Riley, I didn't . . . ," I say.

"Shut up!" Riley says. Alexis releases another loud sob, and Riley's face twists. She whirls around to face her.

"None of us feel sorry for you!" she yells. "You deserve to suffer. You're a *monster*."

Something in Alexis snaps when Riley screams that last word at her. The light drains from her eyes, leaving her skin hollow and pale. The final sob dies on her lips, and her mouth hangs open—shocked.

"Lexie." Grace takes a step toward her, but Alexis pushes herself to her feet and races from the room. The rickety ladder shakes and moans as she climbs to the second floor.

"You bitch, I told you not to leave." Riley pushes past Grace and tears down the ladder after Alexis. Alexis's sobs echo below us. Her bare feet slap against the floor as she drops from the ladder and starts to run.

"Should we go after them?" Grace asks.

As an answer, I head for the ladder. I shouldn't be so worried. Alexis has been almost as bad as Riley this whole time. She put her sister in a coma. I should leave the two of them together—they deserve each other.

Still, I can't get Alexis's broken expression out of my mind.

Riley drops to the floor, causing the ladder to shake. I grip the banister to keep from falling.

"You're as bad as Brooklyn!" Riley shouts, tearing down the hallway. "Maybe we should exorcise you next."

My heart thuds in my chest as my shoe slips on a blood-coated rung. I smack my chin on the ladder before managing to catch myself. Black stars blossom before my eyes.

"Get back here, psycho!" Riley trips over a beer bottle and falls, hitting the ground on her knees. Alexis races into the master bedroom. Riley pushes herself back to her feet.

"Riley, wait!" Stomach turning, I jump to the second floor. The shock jolts through my legs, but I don't pause long enough to notice. I reach for Riley's shoulder, but she whips around on me.

"This has nothing to do with you," she spits out, pushing me. I slam against the wall.

"Riley," I groan, but she follows Alexis into the master bedroom and shuts the door in my face. I grab the doorknob, but it won't turn. Grace runs up behind me, breathless.

"Locked," I say. "From the inside."

Grace wiggles the doorknob, but it holds tight. She swears under her breath, then pounds against the door with her open hand.

"Riley! Let us in."

No one answers. I picture Riley pushing Brooklyn below the water in the bathtub, Riley peeling away Brooklyn's fingernail and letting it fall to the floor in the basement.

"Riley wouldn't hurt Alexis, right?" I ask.

Grace swallows and presses her lips together. "I don't know what Riley would do."

I press my face against the door to the bedroom. Muffled voices sound inside—more arguing, but I can't hear what they're saying. Cursing, I pull away.

"We have to get inside," I say to Grace. "Can you think of anything?"

Grace's face lights up. "Riley kept a key in a drawer in the kitchen. I don't know if it's the master, but . . ."

"It's worth a try," I finish. "Come on." I grab Grace's arm and we start down the stairs.

I take them two at a time, nervous for every second I'm not in the bedroom with Riley and Alexis. I see that desperate, broken expression every time I close my eyes and urge my feet to move faster.

Alexis releases a shrill scream. "Riley, no!"

I jump to the landing as a shadow falls past the arched window overlooking the staircase. Something crashes into the bushes next to the house, sending a shudder through the floor. A thousand pins prick the back of my neck. I freeze on the landing.

"Oh, god." Grace's body stiffens behind me.

"What was that?" I whisper, terrified I already know. I don't want to look, but I turn toward the window anyway and lean into the glass.

Alexis's body lies crumpled in the dirt. Her

white-blond hair glows in the dim moonlight, and a halo of blood pools around her head. I lift a trembling finger to the window, my breath misting the glass.

"Move," I whisper to her broken body. But she doesn't. She stares at the sky with milky, lifeless eyes. Her arm twists above her head, and her fingers curl toward her palm, almost like she tried to grab onto something as she fell. Her cracked lips hang open in a silent scream. Her final words echo through my head. *Riley, no!*

The door above us creaks open, and footsteps pad across the floor. I lift my head as Riley stops at the top of the stairs, her face white as death.

"Alexis jumped," she says.

# CHAPTER TWENTY-ONE

Riley wraps her fingers around the banister at the top of the staircase, her eyes unfocused.

"Our Father who art in heaven," she whispers, barely loud enough to hear. A tear slips over her cheek. "Hallowed be thy name . . ."

"Don't." I step away from the window, hands trembling at my sides. "He's not listening."

"Sofia," Grace murmurs. She tries to touch my arm, but I shake her hand away. I can't stop thinking about Alexis's cloudy eyes, her broken body, the way her fingers curled toward her palm. I don't want to be comforted.

Riley considers me for a long moment, until the anger burning through my chest cools, just a little. "You're grieving," she says finally. "I get that. But we have to pray for the Lord to forgive Alexis's sin."

"No!" I shout. The word is a death sentence, but I don't care. Maybe I want Riley to kill me next. "You're wrong about everything. God's not helping us. He's not fixing Brooklyn, and he can't forgive Alexis, not anymore."

Riley's feet pad down the stairs soundlessly. She crouches in front of me.

"You don't know that, Sof," she says, wiping a tear from her cheek with the back of her hand. "Come back up to the attic. We have to finish what we started."

"The attic?" My voice sounds so shrill I hardly recognize it as my own. I swallow, trying to steady it. "We have to call the police. Alexis is *dead*."

The word sounds so final as it echoes through the house.

Grace sobs into her hands. "Don't say that," she hisses through her fingers. "Maybe she's just . . . just . . ."

"Stop it! Alexis is *dead*, Grace! She committed suicide." Riley's voice caresses that word. *Suicide*. It's like she's trying it out on us, seeing how the story sounds when she says it out loud.

"Think about it," she continues. "What would happen

if we brought the cops here now? What do you think they'll do when they see Brooklyn? They'll think we're *monsters*. I don't want to spend the rest of my life in jail. Do you?"

Grace shakes her head. "Shit," she whispers. She hangs her head and starts to cry, her movements already slow and clumsy from the wine.

Every emotion I've forced down since entering this house explodes out of me. I try to speak, but the most I can do is release a gasping, ugly sob. My chest tightens, and I cry like I'm five years old again, like it's something I just discovered I could do.

"Sofia." Riley grabs me by the shoulder and squeezes. "Sofia, you need to calm down."

I can't stop. I realize, for the first time, that none of us is ever going home. Even if I somehow get out of this house alive, I never get to return to my old life. Tears race down my cheeks as I heave and choke for breath. My head starts to feel fuzzy.

"Sofia, look at me." Suddenly Riley's voice is soft and even. My eyes flutter open, and I focus on her face, my lips trembling as I struggle to breathe.

Riley presses her lips together, considering me. The deep shadows under her eyes make her look older, wise even. She's given up on the ponytail, and now her hair falls limply around her thin, angular face. It hides the bite mark on her cheek, so she looks almost normal. She squeezes my shoulders again.

"I know you don't realize it now, but everything that's happened is Brooklyn's fault," she explains. "The devil compelled Alexis to jump out that window. There's nothing we can do for her now, but you need to be strong—you need to keep the devil from taking control of you, too."

*Keep the devil from taking control of me, too.* The words echo in my head, meaningless, but I still feel my breathing begin to steady.

"There's my girl," she whispers. "Now, don't worry. As soon as we beat this, we can all go home."

"How?" I whisper. Riley wipes a tear from my cheek with her thumb. My skin burns where she touches it, but I try not to let my disgust show on my face. The only way out of here is through Riley. I have to be strong.

"We'll figure it out. Some exorcisms are just trickier than others." Riley stands, smoothing her bloodstained tank top. "Take a moment to catch your breath, then come back to the attic. All three of us need to be united if this is going to work. We might have to resort to extreme measures to defeat the demon."

I nod numbly as Riley turns and walks back up the stairs and down the hallway. Grace crouches near the wall, so still she looks like a shadow.

"Are you ready?" Grace asks. I don't think I'll ever be ready to go back up there, but I push myself to my feet and take a step toward her. She wraps a hand around my arm, and we walk down the hall together.

"What do you think Riley meant when she said extreme measures?" I ask before we reach the stairs to the attic. Grace blinks at me blearily. Her eyes are clouded over, and she can barely walk straight. When she speaks, her voice is raspy, almost a whisper.

"She meant that sometimes the host has to die."

# CHAPTER TWENTY-TWO

"Jesus, Sofia, *go*." Grace pinches my leg, and the jolt of pain gets me moving. I climb up the last three ladder rungs, then pull myself into the attic. The room itself feels evil, like something twisted crawled into the spaces Alexis left behind.

Riley stares out the window at the far end of the room, one arm angled in front of her. Rope coils around her feet. I peer around the beam. Brooklyn lies, twisted, on the floor, her arms and legs untied. Her spiky blond hair is slicked with blood.

The attic door slams shut behind me. I whirl around in time to see Grace stand and wipe her dusty hands on her jeans.

"What's going on?" I ask. Grace shifts her eyes to the floor.

Moonlight streams through the window, leaving the attic thick with shadows. I don't see what Riley's holding until she steps forward and candlelight illuminates her hands.

The nail gun.

*Sometimes the host has to die.* Just a few hours ago I'd have done anything to stop this. But now I hesitate, curling my fingers into fists. It's Brooklyn's life or mine. By helping her, I make myself Riley's next target.

Brooklyn whimpers and tries to sit up.

"Almost done," Riley says. She shifts the nail gun to one hand, then drops to her knees and rolls Brooklyn onto her back.

"Don't, please!" Brooklyn writhes and kicks beneath Riley's legs. Riley lowers the nail gun.

I can't do this. I can't stand by and watch someone die, even if it means saving myself.

"Get off of her!" I throw my whole body into Riley, using every ounce of strength I have left. "You psycho bitch!"

We tumble to the floor next to Brooklyn. Riley regains her balance first and whips an elbow into my face. I slam back down, pain exploding across my cheek.

"Grace, take care of her," Riley snarls. Brooklyn tries to move, but Riley straddles her chest and pins her arm to the floor with one hand. I push myself up and try to crawl toward them, but Grace grabs me from behind.

"Let go!" I claw at Grace's arms, but she just tightens her grip around my chest and drags me away. Splinters jutting out from the unfinished wooden floor scrape the backs of my legs.

An eerie silence fills the attic. Riley lowers the gun. The nail shoots into Brooklyn's hand with a dull blast, breaking the quiet.

Brooklyn roars with pain, so loud I swear I feel the floorboards tremble beneath my feet. Riley moves to the next arm, pinning it beneath her knee as she positions the nail gun over Brooklyn's hand. It sticks straight out from her body, like a cross.

"You're crucifying her," I whisper, horrified. A thick line of blood oozes over the side of Brooklyn's hand and pools on the floor.

She aims the gun at Brooklyn's other palm and pulls the trigger. Metal crunches through skin and bone.

"I wanted to hang her from the beams," Riley explains, motioning to the ceiling with the nail gun. "But I didn't think we could lift her that high." She curls her toes into the floor and pivots around to face me.

"Now, what should we do with you?" she says, almost to herself. She raises an eyebrow, and suddenly it's as if all the air in the room has been sucked away.

"No, please," I beg. Grace tightens her grip around my arms, and I can't move.

"It's for your own good," Riley says, gathering the ropes she'd used to tie up Brooklyn. "First you texted Josh, and then you played that little trick with the wine. Now this. I just don't trust you anymore."

"Please," I whisper again, trying to pull out of Grace's grip. "I can cooperate. I can help."

Riley untangles a length of rope as she moves toward me. She lifts a finger to her lips.

"This'll be easier if you don't struggle," she says. As Grace holds me in place, Riley binds my arms and legs in thick knots. The ropes pinch the skin around my wrists, and they're so tight they cut off circulation in my hands. When she's done, Riley pushes the hair out of my face and leans in to kiss me on the cheek.

"When we're done with Brooklyn, we'll help you. Okay?" She taps my nose with her finger. "It's almost dawn. Grace and I need to do something with Alexis's body before the sun comes up."

I turn to the window and see that Riley's right. The black sky has faded to a deep blue. I think of my mother crawling out of bed at seven in the morning as always and finding my room empty. A spark of hope flickers through my chest—if she calls the police, then maybe . . . but no. Even if she called 911 as soon as she found me missing, they'd never find me here. Not in time to stop Riley.

Grace pushes my shoulders down, and I awkwardly sit. "Riley," I try one last time. "Please don't leave me here like this."

Riley ignores my pleas as she opens the attic door and starts down the ladder.

Grace hesitates at the door. "It's easier this way," she says. Without another word she follows Riley down to the second floor.

I release my breath in a rush of air. *It's easier.* Karen said that to me once, after watching Lila and Erin torture me in biology class. *It's just easier to let them do what they want.* What bullshit.

I struggle to keep myself calm, but as reality sets in, each breath feels more ragged. I squeeze my eyes closed, and the situation comes into clearer focus. Riley knows I'm not on her side, that I can't be trusted. Alexis is dead. Soon, Brooklyn will be, too. Maybe Riley will decide I'm possessed, too. Maybe I'll be the next person nailed to the floor.

Tears stream down my cheeks. I'm crying for Alexis and for Brooklyn, but also for myself—for fear of what's going to happen next. I release another sob, no longer trying to keep my pain under control. My shoulders shake, and my chest aches as my breathing gets heavier and heavier. Tears cloud my eyes until I can barely see.

"Stop!" Brooklyn screams. Her voice startles me so much that I dig my teeth into my lower lip, sniffling. Brooklyn groans in pain, and there's a shuffling sound as she tries to readjust her position on the floor. "This isn't the time to cry. We need to figure out how to escape."

"Escape? I've been trying to escape since we first got here!" I press my lips together to keep from sobbing again. "There *is* no escape."

"Bullshit. We've just been thinking about this wrong." Brooklyn pauses, and for a moment the only sound in the attic is her low, steady breathing. "What's Riley been saying this whole time?"

"That . . . that you're evil." I stutter. "That you're possessed by the devil."

"Right. And what would the devil do in this situation?"

The words flash into my head, and I say them without thinking. "Fight fire with fire."

There's a beat of silence. Then Brooklyn says, "Exactly."

# CHAPTER TWENTY-THREE

The words repeat in my head: *Fight fire with fire*. It's not exactly a solution. My arms and legs are bound so tightly I can hardly move, and Brooklyn is nailed to the floor. There's no way for us to fight. It's over.

Still, I keep replaying those words, like something about that sentence can unlock the secret to escape. Brooklyn is oddly quiet, and I wonder if she's doing the same thing. Or maybe she's already figured out a plan of her own.

Wind presses against the far window, and the glass groans. There's only one candle still lit—the thick white one Alexis brought up here. Its flame flickers, like it's mocking me.

Giggles echo through the floor below us, then the ladder creaks. I shoot a fearful look at the door. Riley and Grace are back.

"Brooklyn," I whisper.

"I hear them." Brooklyn groans, and the rough soles of her boots scratch the floor as she moves her legs. "It's okay. We have a plan, remember?"

"Fight fire with fire," I whisper. The words echo through my head, meaning nothing to me. *Fight fire with fire. Fight fire with fire.*

The attic door shudders and falls open with a slap that makes the floor tremble. Still burning, the last candle topples over and rolls to the wall, coming to a stop against a bit of exposed pink insulation. I watch it happen as if it's a dream.

The flame leaps to the wall and licks the raw wood hungrily.

"Brooklyn, did you see that?" I can't see Brooklyn's face, just the blood-coated soles of her boots. She taps them together, like Dorothy. Time to go home.

"All part of our plan," she says.

*What plan?* I want to scream at her. All we had were words—words that definitely don't have the power to knock over a candle.

But as the fire spreads, it burns the question from my mind. The very small, very *wooden* attic I'm trapped in is going up in flames. I yank against the ropes binding me in place. Smoke seeps into my mouth and presses against the back of my throat.

Riley appears at the attic door as smoke clouds the far corner and rises to the ceiling, thick and dark. She grimaces and waves a hand in front of her face.

"What the hell?" she mutters.

Brooklyn snickers, her laughter bouncing off the burning walls. I stare at her boots, shocked. She's lost her mind.

Riley hovers on the ladder, the flames reflected in her eyes. Grace's hysterical voice echoes below, but I can't make out what she's saying. Footsteps slam against the floor as Grace runs away.

"Riley!" I shout. "You have to untie me!" The ropes rub away the top layer of skin around my wrists as I twist and pull against them. I hardly even notice the pain. A flicker of orange appears in my peripheral vision, eating its way closer to me. I take shaky breath after shaky breath, ignoring the smoke coating my mouth and tongue. "Riley, you have to let us out. Riley!"

Riley presses herself against the attic door, searching the floor for something to suffocate the fire. But there's nothing up here except for the discarded toolbox. Even the bottle of holy water is empty.

"Help! Help us, please!"

Riley's shoulders tense. She shifts her eyes to me.

"Don't," I beg her. All around me, the fire presses in. It takes every ounce of willpower I have not to imagine it crawling over my skin, eating away my hair and my fingernails until there's nothing left. "Don't leave me. *Please*."

But Riley's eyes glaze over, until it no longer seems like she sees me. "The exorcism . . ." she says.

"It doesn't matter anymore," I say. Blue tendrils stretch over the wood, reaching for us like fingers. I tug my legs apart, trying to loosen the ropes at my ankles. But they hold tight.

"You can't leave us here!" I shout. Of all the ways I thought I might die in this house, burning alive is the most cruel. "You can't!"

Riley hesitates. There's a loud crack, and a ceiling beam splits in half and swings to the floor, spraying sparks as it falls. The tiny embers land on my arms and legs and eat through my jeans, stinging my skin.

"Oh, god," I beg, squeezing my eyes shut. "You can't leave us here."

Riley's face turns white, and her lower lip trembles. "Lord, forgive me," she whispers. Her head disappears as she ducks out of the attic, the ladder creaking beneath her weight.

"No! *No!*" I scream for so long that my voice goes

hoarse. Smoke fills my lungs, and my sobs dissolve in a fit of coughing. The air around us thickens. It clouds my head when I breathe it in, making me feel dizzy and sick to my stomach. We're never getting out of here. We're going to burn to death. We're going to die screaming as flames eat away our faces.

Fire crackles, and another wooden beam drops to the floor. It crashes in the corner, lighting more of Riley's tower of *Vogue* magazines on fire as it sparks. I cough and cough, unable to catch my breath as I watch the flames grow and move.

"Sofia," Brooklyn says, her voice eerily steady, "we can get out of here, but you need to help me."

I choke back my sobs, but I can't slow my rapidly beating heart. "How?" I ask, my voice shaking.

"Can you walk?"

I clumsily try to stand, but my legs are angled in front of me, and without using my arms I can't keep my balance. "No."

"Then crawl if you have to," Brooklyn insists. "Crawl to me. Hurry!"

*Crawl.* I breathe in and then out, focusing on that one word. The fire is so close that I can feel its heat flickering at my ankle, but Brooklyn's not far away. I can make it to her before the fire reaches me. I push past the fears growing in the back of my head. I can crawl. I *will* crawl.

I rock my weight to the left and bite back a groan when my shoulder crashes into the floor. Now I'm lying on my side, my legs curled next to me. Brooklyn's boots are two or three feet away. With my arms still tied behind my back, I can't use them to pull myself, so I dig my heels into the floorboards and scoot across the attic. The fire reaches Riley's nail polish and the bottles explode in a burst of colorful glass, showering me with sparks.

My shoulder aches as I push it over the floor, past Brooklyn's combat boots and blood-and-soot-covered legs. I push myself farther, and then I'm beside her arm.

"What do I do?" I gasp when I'm close enough to see her face. She turns her head so she can look at me. In the crackling orange light, her eyes glow red.

"You need to get the nails out." Brooklyn cringes, and the skin around her eyes crinkles. "You'll have to use your teeth."

Teeth. If I stop and think about what I'm about to do, there's no way I'll go through with it. So I don't think. I rock my body to the side until I roll onto my chest. I pull my knees up, using my forehead to balance my weight against the floor. Brooklyn steadies me with one leg, and I pull myself up to a crouch. I edge myself closer to Brooklyn's hand.

The nail is wedged deep into her palm, and

everything—her skin, her fingernails, the nail itself—is coated in a thick layer of blood. I lower my face to her hand and work my mouth around the nail head. Brooklyn gasps as my teeth scrape over her skin. I bite down on the nail and pull.

The nail digs into my teeth and gums, but it doesn't move. Blood fills my mouth, and it tastes sharp, metallic. I don't know whether it's mine or Brooklyn's. Probably both. I try not to breathe it in as I pull again. The nail bites into the enamel of my teeth, and blood trickles down my throat. I start to gag.

"Sofia, come on," Brooklyn says. "You've got this."

I bite down again, this time wiggling the nail head with my teeth before I pull. It comes loose in my mouth, and I rock backward, nearly losing my balance. Brooklyn releases a strangled cry and hugs her now free hand to her chest. Before I can even spit the nail from my mouth, she reaches to her other hand and digs the nail out herself. It clatters to the floor when she pulls it loose.

"Jesus. Fuck!" she screams, sitting. Fire crackles around us, and the smoke is so thick I can barely make out Brooklyn's face. "Come here," she says to me. "Hurry!"

I move toward her so she can untie the ropes at my wrists. The fire grows around us. Between Brooklyn's bloody hands and the heat of the fire making us sweat, the rope is slick and hard for her to handle. Twice, it slips through Brooklyn's fingers.

Fear beats at my skull. *We're not going to make it*, I think. But then Brooklyn tugs the knots around my wrists loose, and I'm free.

I help her untie the ropes around my ankles, then stumble to my feet, not entirely sure how long the floor will hold. Fire moves over the walls and eats the wood. My eyes sting. I blink, but I can't clear the smoke away. Tears stream down my cheeks. My terror hardens into determination. I'm not dying here. I refuse to die here.

We make it to the next floor seconds before the fire leaps to the top rung of the ladder. Brooklyn doubles over, coughing so hard I worry she'll vomit.

"You can't stop." I grab her arm and pull her toward the stairs. My heart beats in my ears, counting every second that passes. The fire is traveling too fast. It's chasing at our heels, blocking every exit. I'm not sure how much time we have left.

Smoke billows around us, filling my lungs. I pull my shirt over my face, but it doesn't help. My chest aches for air, but every breath I take is toxic. I start to choke, and then I can't stop. My entire body shakes with coughing. Brooklyn straightens and pushes herself down the steps. I slide her arm over my shoulder to help her.

We make our way to the first floor and down the hall.

When we turn the corner, relief floods my body. The door hangs open. I start to run.

The stairs cave in with a crash like thunder, and the smoke is so thick I can barely see. I tighten my arm around Brooklyn and push myself forward. We cross the front porch and make our way down the stairs.

I drop to my knees on the ground, and Brooklyn collapses next to me. For a moment I just rest my forehead against the cool grass, gulping down fresh air. Behind us, the fire licks and crackles and spits. Listening to it, I sit back up and look around.

The sidewalk and road are empty. Riley and Grace are long gone. I swallow the bile that rises in my throat as I picture them stumbling out of the house, ignoring my screams. But I can't think of that now. We don't have a lot of time. This part of the neighborhood might be abandoned, but eventually the smoke will stretch high enough that someone will see and call the police. And then . . .

I turn to Brooklyn, surprised to see she's already watching me. Her black eyes reflect the light of the fire. She pushes herself to her feet and offers me her hand. Once I'm standing, she pulls me close to her and leans in to whisper in my ear.

"Tell no one." Her breath smells like blood and smoke. She steps away from me, then nods once. Without another word, she starts to limp away.

For a long moment I stand there, watching the house burn. I laugh out loud, and the sound is so shocking and wonderful that my eyes well with tears. I didn't die. It's over. I'm free.

The fire moves through the house like a living thing—wild and desperate and hungry. By the time it's done, all the evidence of last night will be destroyed. I think about what Brooklyn said—*tell no one*. If we go to the cops, it'll be her word against Riley's.

I swallow and turn away from the fire. Then I head down the sidewalk, toward home.

# CHAPTER TWENTY-FOUR

My front door creaks open, and I step into the hallway, listening. Silence. Mom isn't out of bed yet. I hold the knob to keep it from clicking and ease the door closed without a sound. I slip my sneakers off and carry them up the stairs so she won't hear my footsteps on the carpet.

I spent the entire walk home debating what I would tell my mom. I want to blurt out the whole story, but Brooklyn's words echo through my head, warning me. *Tell no one.* Besides, if I tell her, she'll just call the cops, and they'll ask questions I'm not sure how to answer. Best to just pretend nothing happened.

I make my way to the bathroom and turn the shower on as hot as it will go. I strip down, and my clothes fall to the floor in a heap of blood and smoke and sweat. I shiver as I stare down at the faded pockets of my jeans, then kick them away from me. I should burn them.

Turning this thought over in my head, I step into the shower—gasping when the hot water hits me. It's painful at first, but as the water runs over my skin, I start to relax. It stings the raw patches of my arms where the ropes rubbed my wrists, and the mangled cuts around my knuckles burn as water soaks the dead skin, washing away clotted blood and dirt. I tilt my head back and fill my mouth with water, then spit it out to get the blood off my teeth and tongue. The water circling the drain is stained a deep, muddy red. I watch it slip away, feeling the horrors of the night disappearing down the drain with it.

*Nothing happened*, I remind myself. It was a nightmare, that's all.

Somewhere in the house a door opens, then shuts. I freeze. I wrap my fingers around the shower curtain, trying to remember whether I locked the front door.

"Sofia?" my mom calls. "Are you up already?"

I shut off the shower and hurriedly dry myself off. I don't remember ever feeling so relieved to hear my mother's voice.

"Just taking a shower." I duck out of the bathroom and into my bedroom, where I quickly change into fresh clothes. I grab a plain white T-shirt, jeans, and my faded gray hooded sweatshirt. Since burning them isn't really an option, I roll my dirty clothes into a ball and shove them all the way to the bottom of the trash can beneath my desk.

I step into the hallway, tugging my sleeves down over my hands so Mom won't see the raw skin at my knuckles. Mom is easing Grandmother's door shut. She glances over her shoulder at me, lifting a finger to her mouth to tell me to keep quiet.

"She's still sleeping," she says. I cross my arms over my chest, cringing when my torn fingers brush against the fabric of my sweatshirt. My mom cocks her head, considering me.

"Are you okay?" she asks. "It's so early. I'm surprised you're awake."

I nod. "I'm fine," I say, but the word cracks in my mouth. Tears pool in my eyes. I try to blink them away, but they spill onto my cheeks. So much for pretending nothing happened.

"Sofia?" My mom crosses the hall and folds me into a hug. For a moment I just let her hold me. The tears come faster, until I'm crying so hard my shoulders shake. Mom smoothes the still damp hair off my forehead.

"Shh," she says. "Shh, it's okay. Tell me what happened."

"I . . ." I choke back my sobs and pull away from her, drying my tears with the sleeves of my sweatshirt. "I just heard that a friend of mine committed suicide." I stare at my bare feet, certain Mom will know I'm lying if I meet her eyes.

"Oh, Sofia." Mom pulls me to her chest again, resting her chin on top of my head. She rubs a hand over my back in slow, comforting circles. "Honey, I'm so sorry."

I close my eyes, allowing myself to relax into her. For the first time in days, I feel safe.

\* \* \*

Fifteen minutes later I'm perched on a stool in the kitchen, the heavy smell of French toast filling the air. I actually smile as I breathe it in. Mom's never been the best cook, but she's perfected her French toast over the years. She uses only the thickest, crustiest bread and always mixes brown sugar and a pinch of cinnamon into the batter. She takes the frying pan off the stove and slides the toast onto a plate.

"I know it's been hard to make friends," she says, pulling the maple syrup and butter from the fridge. "And after what happened at your last school . . ." She shakes her head, and under her breath, she mutters, "Such a needless tragedy."

I shift uncomfortably on my stool and push the French toast around on my plate. I don't want to think about what happened at my last school, not when my wrists are still raw from Riley's ropes. But now that Mom's brought it up, I can't help seeing the similarities. Both times I thought I knew someone, I thought she was my friend, and in the end I was wrong.

Maybe there's a reason these things keep happening to me. Maybe I'm defective.

Mom sets the pan in the sink and crosses over to me, brushing one of my damp curls aside. "But you can't give up, *mija*. I believe in you," she says. "I know you'll find your way."

It's the exact right thing to say at the exact right moment, and I blink furiously to keep from crying. Mom places the plate on the counter in front of me, and I cover the toast in a thick stream of syrup. I can't give up.

* * *

I stay awake for as long as I can, but by noon my eyes are so heavy I can barely keep them open. I tell Mom I'm not feeling well and crawl into bed, falling asleep as soon as I pull the comforter up over my shoulders. While I sleep, I dream.

*Riley and I are sitting on the train tracks, passing a bottle of red wine back and forth. Red-and-orange light bleeds into the sky. Clouds race above us, their shadows flickering over Riley's face. Her skin turns dark, then light again. The ground below us trembles—a train's coming.*

*"Truth or dare," Riley says. She looks perfect, like she did the first day I met her. Her hair pools around her shoulders in flawless spirals, her eyebrows arch high above her eyes. Her cheeks burn pink, so glossy she doesn't look real. The strange light makes everything about her glow. She takes a drink, and a thick drop of wine oozes out of the bottle and over her chin.*

*"Dare," I say. Riley lowers the bottle, but it's not Riley anymore—it's Brooklyn. Black liner surrounds her eyes, making them look too large for her head. The wine running over her chin thickens. Not wine—blood.*

*"Why not truth?" she ask. The train's headlight flickers through the trees behind her.*

*"We have to go." I stand, reaching for Brooklyn's arm. The train flashes its lights. "Brooklyn!"*

*I grab her hand, but it's not Brooklyn—it's Karen. Blood drips from her mouth and coats her teeth.*

*"Why can't you tell the truth?" she asks. The train's horn blares. It sounds like a scream.*

The screaming horn echoes in my head, and I jerk awake. Outside, the only sounds are the wind pushing against the glass in my windows and the low buzz of the cicadas in the grass.

It was just the dream, I tell myself. A nightmare. My eyelids grow heavy, and I'm just about to drift back to sleep when I hear it again—a shrill, terrified scream.

I sit straight up in bed. Hands shaking, I reach over to my bedside table and flip on the lamp. It's getting dark outside. I must have slept all day.

I force one leg out of bed, then the other. I jerk at every shadow, certain it's Riley. But the halls are empty. Downstairs, the front door is closed tight. Everything is still, quiet. Unnerving.

"Hello?" I whisper, but there's no answer. I step forward and open the front door.

Fluorescent red and orange light streaks across the sky. It's that eerie in-between light, neither night nor day. Just like in my dream. I hesitate near the door, wondering if I'm still asleep. Heat presses on my arms and gathers beneath my thick hair. A bead of sweat trickles down the back of my neck. This is too real to be a dream.

"Mom?" I say, stepping onto the porch. She should still be awake. It's probably only seven thirty or eight o'clock. But the street in front of our house is eerily quiet—deserted. After what happened last night, I'm more aware of the emptiness. There's no one here to see where I'm going, no one to hear my screams.

I step, barefoot, onto the dry grass. It crunches beneath my weight, poking the soles of my feet.

"Mom?" I call again, making my way around the side of our house. Our driveway curves off the main street and back behind our house, to an old shed. The sun-warmed pavement burns the bottoms of my feet. Insects buzz in the yard, but the sound is so familiar to me that I almost don't notice it.

The red-lit sky casts shadows over the driveway. I move slowly, easing around Mom's giant black SUV.

A shadow streaks across the driveway and I freeze, biting back a scream. Then my eyes focus, and I make out a squirrel crouched beneath a bush. I breathe a sigh of relief.

The smell reaches me first, the same heavy, sick scent I noticed beneath the bleachers on my first day of school. Chicken after a night in the garbage. Fish left in the heat. I picture the skinned cat, and my skin prickles. Trembling, I walk around the car.

There's another sound now, a dripping. My skin pricks, warning me. I should run. Instead, I move closer.

Thick white candles line the sides of the driveway, their wicks flickering in the twilight. A hastily painted black pentagram stretches across the driveway beneath them, and in the middle of the star lies a dark black pool.

*Drip. Drip. Drip.*

I look up.

A human body hangs from the shed, its arms stretched out to either side and tied to the roof gutters with thick rope. The body doesn't look remotely human anymore. Its skin has been peeled back in strips, revealing the pink muscle and blood and tissue beneath.

The only parts of the body that are still intact are its hands and its feet. My eyes hover at its feet. From the feet hang Grace's gold platform sandals.

I gasp and throw my hands over my mouth. Grace's head lolls forward unnaturally, and her lifeless, cloudy eyes stare at the ground. Someone shaved off her hair, leaving behind a bloody scalp. Her arms stretch to either side, like she's been crucified. Blood drips from her body.

"Grace!" I shriek. There's not a person on earth who could survive what her body's been through, but I stumble toward her anyway. "Oh my god, Grace! Grace, no!"

I trip over one of the candles and fall, hard. The driveway peels back the top layer of skin on my knee. I cringe and try to push myself to my feet. The candle sputters out as it topples onto the asphalt.

In the candle's last glimmer of light, I see movement below Grace's body. I freeze. Brooklyn crouches in the shadows, her head ducked so that, at first, all I see is her spiky blond hair. She stands slowly, her eyes leveled on me. She steps into the circle of candlelight.

"Fun fact," she says. "We're not really afraid of fire."

She smiles, a pocketknife clenched in her hand. The candlelight surrounding her flickers, making the knife's blade glint.

"Brooklyn," I start, but the words I want to say get caught in my throat. I picture Grace jumping out from behind my bench to scare me on my second day of school. Grace, who wore leopard-print headbands and sequin skirts and got so excited about her crush on Tom. She must've felt the same relief I did when she ran out of the house this morning. She must've thought that whole terrible night was finally behind her. And now she's dead.

Not just dead—mutilated. Tortured. Bile rises in my throat. I clench my eyes shut, but Grace's body stays painted on the insides of my lids. Her skin curling away from her limbs. Her scalp, bald and bloody.

I open my eyes again. Brooklyn crouches and lowers her finger to the pool of Grace's blood, then lifts it to her mouth. Her grin widens as she runs her tongue up the side of her finger, licking the blood away. She stands, tightening her grip on the knife. My fear sharpens, and I stumble backward, banging into the back door to the house.

Behind me, the door creaks open. I whirl around as my mom steps outside.

"Sofia?" she says, groggily. "What's going on? I heard noises."

I glance over my shoulder, but Brooklyn's gone. My voice freezes in my throat.

"Mom," I start. "I . . ."

Before I can think of what to say, my mom's eyes shift to the body hanging from the shed. The blood drains from her face, and she screams.

# CHAPTER TWENTY-FIVE

"**M**om?" A tremor begins in my hand, then spreads up my arm until my whole body shakes. I did this. I trusted Brooklyn, I let her out. The sharp, metallic taste of her blood still lingers on my tongue. Riley told me she was evil, but I didn't listen. What happened to Grace happened because of me.

I put a hand on my mom's arm and she stiffens, finally dropping her hands from her mouth.

"Get inside. Lock all the doors and call the police." Her voice is quiet, but there's steel behind her words. She's Sergeant Nina Flores now, medical technician for the armed forces, and this is just another fallen soldier.

She rolls up her sleeves and starts down the porch steps. "I'll get her . . . I'll get it down."

I hesitate. I don't want to leave my mother outside alone. Brooklyn could be lurking behind a bush or parked car.

"Sofia, now!" Mom's tone leaves no room for argument. I cast one last look at Grace's broken body, then race back inside and stumble upstairs for my cell phone. My hands are sweating when I reach my bedroom, and I mess up the three-digit number twice and have to start over.

Finally, "Nine-one-one, what's your emergency?" a robotic voice asks on the other end of the line.

"I . . ." I swallow. "My friend's been . . ." I don't know what to say. Mutilated? Tortured? Skinned? I swallow. "My friend's been killed. Please come."

I give them my address, then hang up the phone. For a long moment I stare down at it, stunned. Riley was right. The reality of that hits me, and I almost can't breathe. She was right all along—Brooklyn's possessed. She killed Mr. Willis. And now she's killed Grace. If my mother hadn't come along, she would have killed me.

Maybe she should have killed me. Maybe I deserve that.

"*Diablo.*"

I freeze, shocked to hear my grandmother's voice for the first time in years.

*Diablo*—devil.

I walk to my bedroom door, my cell phone clenched in my hand. The thick carpet in the hallway muffles my footsteps, and the red-tinted lamp from Grandmother's bedroom casts the only light. A violent, hacking cough rattles behind her door. It sounds like death.

I ease one foot into the hallway, searching the shadows around me for the outline of a body. I can't blink without picturing Brooklyn holding that pocketknife, Brooklyn dipping her finger into the pool of Grace's blood—then licking it off. *Your fault*, my brain whispers to me. *Your fault*.

I push the images and accusations away. The shadows seem to move around me, but I know it's just my imagination. Brooklyn isn't here.

Grandmother's face looks like a melting candle. Her skin droops so badly that it's difficult to pick out her features. Her rosary beads click against her table. She releases a rough, raw-sounding cough.

"Grandmother?" I hover near her door, almost afraid to go inside. Grandmother inhales. The sound is like a crumpling paper bag. She moves her thumb along the row of beads.

"Are you okay?"

Grandmother turns her head very slowly. The rosary beads shake in her fragile, trembling hands.

"*Diablo*," she whispers. A shiver creeps down my spine. She hasn't spoken since her stroke. The doctors weren't even sure she *could* speak anymore.

She focuses her cloudy eyes on me. It's like she's looking through me.

"*Diablo*," she says.

"It was an accident," I hiss.

"*Diablo*," Grandmother says, like a prayer.

"It wasn't my fault. It was an accident, just like last time." The words rush out of my mouth before I can think about them.

"*Diablo!*"

I look past Grandmother, to the Virgin statuette on her windowsill. It glows white in the red-tinted room. Grandmother used to tell me confession absolved you of guilt. By admitting our sins before God, we are no longer held responsible for them. God takes the blame from us. He makes us pure again.

More than anything in the world right now, I want to be pure. My dream echoes through my head. I hear the roaring train race down the tracks, and Karen's distant voice. *Why can't you tell the truth?*

I drop to my knees next to Grandmother's bed and fold my hands in prayer.

"Blessed Mary, mother of God," I whisper. "Forgive me for I have sinned."

I close my eyes, and I'm at the party with Karen, humiliated and crying.

*I stagger when I push my way out of the party and reach the porch. I almost expect the other kids to chase after me, throwing more Q-tips. But they don't. They're probably too drunk.*

*I'm not entirely sure where to go next. I don't want to go home—it'd be too humiliating seeing my mom and grandmother after this. Tears prick my eyes and spill onto my cheeks.*

*Then the high-pitched sound of the train horn blares through the night, followed by the distant roar of an engine. I stumble down the porch steps and into the backyard. It's dark, but the train's headlight flickers through the trees. I start to run.*

*The sound calms me. It's so loud, so all encompassing that I can't think of anything else. I step out of the trees and into the clearing just before the train tracks. Adrenaline fills my blood, making me reckless. The laugher and the Q-tips are far away now, almost like they happened to someone else. Like they were a dream.*

*The train's headlight shines through the trees as it curves around. Without thinking, I step onto the tracks. They shudder and quake beneath my sneakers. I close my eyes, and the world fades away. It's just me, the shaking earth, and the thunderous noise.*

*"Sofia!" My eyes snap open, and I turn to see Karen stumble through the trees. She's still holding her beer. As she runs toward me, the foamy liquid sloshes over the side and spills to the ground. "What are you doing?"*

*"What does it look like?" My eyes linger on Karen's face long enough to see the blood drain from her skin, and her eyes widen with shock. Good. After what she did, she deserves to be afraid. I turn back around. I want to face the train head on. The light moves closer.*

*Karen stops a few feet away from the tracks. "Jesus! It was just a joke."*

*"A joke?" I say. "How funny do you think it'll be when they find my body tomorrow and everyone blames you?"*

*The tracks tremble violently beneath my feet. It's almost hard to keep my balance, like I'm standing on the high dive and peering over the side, preparing to jump. The train honks again, and a wave of doubt crashes over me. What am I doing? I don't want to die.*

*Karen's face crumples. She drops her beer and grabs my arm. "Sofia, get off the tracks!"*

*Her cold fingers tighten around my wrist, disgusting me. Maybe I don't want to die, but the alternative—letting Karen save me, going back to the party where I was humiliated—is even worse.*

*I blink into the headlight, frozen. It's close enough now that I can't look at it directly. . . .*

"Karen jumped in front of the train," I whisper in Grandmother's red-tinted bedroom. "She pushed me off the tracks. She . . . she saved my life." I sniff and reach for Grandmother's hand. "And it killed her."

Lights flash from the window, painting the Virgin red and blue. I cross Grandmother's room and push the curtains aside. An ambulance pulls up to the curb. Paramedics leap out and race for Grace's lifeless body.

I step back, and the curtain slides back into place. Grandmother stares at me with those glassy eyes and slowly raises a finger.

"*Diablo* . . ." she croaks. My skin prickles with horror, not at what she's saying, but at the rasping emptiness of her voice. It's not my grandmother speaking anymore. The voice doesn't even sound human.

"*Diablo* . . ." she says, pointing at me. I back away from her bed.

"Grandmother, no," I say. But she's right. I let Brooklyn go, so Grace's death is my fault, just as much as Karen's is. If Brooklyn gets to Riley, I'll be responsible for that, too.

I feel like I'm standing on the tracks again, blinking into the headlight of the oncoming train. But this time I know exactly what to do. I can't be responsible for another girl's death, even if it's Riley's. I have to find her before Brooklyn does, and I have to save her life. It's the only way I'll ever be able to forgive myself for the blood already on my hands. It's the only way God will ever forgive me.

I turn, stumbling as I race from the room. Grandmother's whispery voice follows me down the stairs.

*"Diablo . . . Diablo!"*

# CHAPTER TWENTY-SIX

I slip out the back door so Mom doesn't see me leave. I don't have time to explain this to her, not when Riley's in danger. I ease the door shut and hurry, barefoot, across the yard. The dewy grass chills my feet, so I stop at the garage and pull on my mom's gardening boots. Then I start to run.

I call Riley three times, but she doesn't answer. I'm out of breath when I reach her driveway.

Riley's palatial house towers over me, its windows dark. I imagine the worst: Riley's body crumpled and broken inside the house. Brooklyn standing above her, blood dripping from the pocketknife clenched in her fingers. The horrors cycle through my head as I walk up to the house.

Perfectly trimmed bushes line her driveway. The garden hose is tied up neatly, not a kink in sight. A handmade WELCOME sign hangs on the front door. This is all wrong. Riley's family doesn't deserve this. Brooklyn can't destroy their picturesque life.

A curtain in one of the windows moves. My heart leaps in my chest.

"Riley?" I stumble up the steps to her porch. I lift my hand and knock on the door. It creaks open beneath my fist.

My whole body tenses. I should run, pretend I was never here. But the second I consider leaving, my grandmother's raspy voice whispers in my ear. *Diablo, Diablo.*

"Riley?" I step into the dark hallway and run my hand along the wall. My fingers find the light switch, and the chandelier hanging from the ceiling blinks on.

A bloody handprint stretches across the wall, like someone dragged their fingers over the paint. Deep gouges scratch into the wood, and the framed photographs lining the foyer hang crooked. Several have fallen to the floor, the glass in their frames spider-webbed with cracks. I take a step closer, narrowing my eyes at them. Someone's drawn bloody smiley faces over the photographs. It looks like a child's finger-painting. In the corner of one, I see the same pentagram symbol that had been drawn on my driveway under Grace's mutilated remains.

Brooklyn's been here.

A dull, buzzing noise echoes in my ears as I walk down the hallway. It's the cicadas outside, just like always. But they sound louder now, closer. The floor beneath my feet seems to tremble, like on the train tracks the night of the party. Any second, my world could come crashing down around me.

"Riley?" I call again. I make my way into the living room, where I find overturned furniture scattered across the floor, a shattered television set, and pillows slashed open. A layer of downy feathers covers the carpet. I kick them up with my boots as I cross the room, studying the damage. The wispy white feathers stick to my jeans and my hands and my hair. They tickle my skin, sending shivers up my arms.

Something drops onto the floor behind me with a thud. I spin around, heart hammering in my chest.

It's just a book. Books have been pulled from all the shelves lining all the walls, their pages ripped from the covers, crumpled and tossed around the destruction like confetti. Brooklyn dragged her knife through the curtains, shredding them. She smashed through windows. Shattered glass glints from the carpet, and warm, sticky air moves what's left of the curtains. Eerie red twilight spills onto the floor, painting the entire room the color of blood and fire.

"Riley?" I leave the living room and head to the staircase. "Riley, are you there?"

I wrap my trembling fingers around the banister. As I climb each stair, they creak beneath my rubber boots. Brooklyn could be hiding inside any of these rooms, carving up Riley's body with her pocketknife like she did Grace. Waiting for me.

My hands shake. I stop in front of the first door and wrap my fingers around the doorknob. *I'm allowed to be afraid*, I remind myself, taking a deep breath of the hot, stale hallway air. I'm just not allowed to run away.

I push the door open.

It's just a coat closet, empty and dark. My shoulders slump, relieved. I reach forward and tug on the metal chain hanging from the ceiling.

The light switches on, glinting off the fresh, bloody handprints covering the walls. The porcelain doll from the attic hangs from the ceiling, a thick rope knotted around its neck. Fire blackened most of her face and burned off her hair. Stuffing pokes through the ripped seams at her arms. Her eye sockets are empty, the cloudy glass eyes long gone.

"*Shout to the . . . Shout to the . . . Shout to the . . .*"

The music blares to life, startling me. I choke back a scream, searching the closet until I see the pink CD player on the top shelf. I stand on tiptoes and yank it down, letting it crash to the floor. Dropping to my knees, I rip open the deck and pull out the CD, flinging it back into the closet. I stand and slam the door shut again, heart racing. I squeeze my eyes closed, collapsing against the wall behind me. It's just a CD player, I tell myself.

I make my way down the hallway one room at a time. I open every single door, steeling myself for what I'll find behind it. I'm greeted with more destruction: a bathroom filled with shredded toilet paper, a guest bedroom empty except for a few broken pieces of furniture.

I save Riley's bedroom for last.

I approach it slowly, like I'd approach a rabid dog or wild animal. I turn the knob all the way around, so the lock won't click when I open it. Then I lean my head against the wood, listening. Silence. At first. Then I hear whispering.

"Riley?" My voice shakes. I push the door all the way open and stumble into the room, preparing myself for what Brooklyn's done.

But Riley's room is perfect: no broken furniture or shattered windows, no blood on the walls. I cross to her vanity table and flick on her lamp. Golden light spills over the scarves and glass bottles lining her vanity table, sending broken fragments of colored light flickering over the wood. It illuminates Riley's porcelain doll's glassy, lifeless eyes and the collage of photographs covering Riley's mirror.

I pause in front of the mirror, running a finger along a photograph's edge. It's a picture of Riley, Grace, and Alexis at the lake house, all of them carefree and happy. When Riley first invited me into her room, I remember wanting my photograph to make it to her mirror collage, wedged between snapshots of Grace and Riley. Now that doesn't seem possible.

I unpeel the picture from the mirror, studying Grace's and Alexis's faces. There's something hideous about their smiles, especially when I think of how they ended up. It's like the world played a cruel joke on them. Still, I slip the photograph into my pocket. Better to remember them like this, the way they were.

I hear it again—whispering.

I slide the photograph into my back pocket and start to turn. Out of the corner of my eye I see Riley's bed reflected in her mirror. I freeze. Someone's there, lying beneath the comforter.

"Riley?" The tension building in my chest suddenly releases. I exhale and race across the room. "Jesus, Riley, I've been yelling for you. Are you okay?"

I fumble for the blanket's edge and pull it back.

Alexis's dead body flops onto its side. The few remaining wispy blond strands of hair attached to her skull flutter away from her face. Blackened flesh bubbles like tar around the hole where her nose is supposed to be, and crispy red flecks of skin stick to the pillowcase. Skin peels away from her cheeks, letting bone and muscle poke through.

Bile rises in my throat, but I can't look away. Alexis's teeth remain intact, but blackened, and fire ate away her lips, leaving her mouth in a permanent snarl. Even her eyes are gone. All that's left are two sunken, empty sockets.

The sound starts again. It's not whispering, not exactly. It sounds more like dull clicking, like fingernails snapping. I freeze, and my stomach turns.

Alexis's mouth drops open.

"Holy shit." I stumble backward, staring. Something moves deep in Alexis's throat. It twitches in the darkness, and a tiny, hairy leg stretches over her teeth.

The cockroach crawls across Alexis's tongue and spills onto her chest. A second clings to the roof of her mouth, antennae twitching. It watches me with glassy black eyes.

Dozens of cockroaches pour out of her mouth and scurry down her body. They nestle into the charred remains of her clothes and dig into her blond hair. A few burrow into her ears. They crawl on top of one another, gushing out of Alexis's nose and mouth and cracks in her skull. An antenna appears in the tissue of her cheek as a cockroach digs through the remaining rotten, weak flesh on her face.

The clicking grows until it's too loud for me to hear anything else. A cockroach creeps over Alexis's burned stub of a chin and hisses. Tissue-thin wings unfold from its back.

I scream until my throat goes raw. I back away from Alexis, trip over a pillow, and drop to my knees. The cockroaches multiply, blanketing the bed. They drip onto the floor in a brown scaly mass. I try to push myself away, but I'm too late. Cockroaches skitter up my fingers and legs. Their tiny legs dig into my arms. They plow into my hair and slip below my clothes. One crawls along the neck of my T-shirt, then falls into my bra, antennae twitching against my skin. Another creeps along the side of my face and hisses in my ear.

I push myself to my feet and race for the door. The floor lamp flickers, sending two-foot-long shadows of cockroaches over the walls. I glance over my shoulder. The insects climb over the lampshade, wings fluttering. They're everywhere now: crawling up the walls and covering the floor. A thick layer of roaches swarms the window, blocking out the moonlight.

I rip the door open and race into the hallway, slamming it behind me. Cockroaches click and hiss behind the wood, and I see their flickering shadows in the inch of space between the door and the carpet. I back up against the opposite wall. My skin itches. I feel them crawling over my body, slipping down my T-shirt, clinging to the back of my neck. I swat at my arms and legs, but my hands come away clean. I close my eyes, exhaling, and collapse against the wall.

Something drips onto my nose. My eyes shoot back open.

The ceiling swells with blood. Thick, tacky drops trickle down on me, coating my hair and shoulders, speckling my face. I push myself away from the wall, and my boots slip on the blood splattered across the hallway as I run for the stairs. I grab the banister to steady myself. A cockroach crawls over my fingers and I scream, shaking it off.

The air moves behind me, and the clicking, hissing cockroaches fall silent. All the hair on the back of my neck sticks straight up.

Someone's there, in the hallway. I can feel her. I imagine Alexis climbing out of Riley's bed, sooty, ashy skin crumbling from her face with every step she takes.

I don't look back over my shoulder. I don't want to know if I'm right.

I take the steps to the first floor two at a time. The ceiling rains blood, and swarms of cockroaches crawl over my rubber boots. The weight of the staircase shifts beneath my feet. I feel that thing behind me, feel it closing in, reaching its raw, burning red hands out to grab me.

I leap down the last three steps and stumble into the foyer, landing on all fours. Glass shards wedge into my knees and bite the palms of my hands. I push myself back to my feet and scramble out the front door, onto the porch.

The sky still burns with eerie light, like it's on fire. It's demon light. The devil's light.

I don't stop running until I reach the curb, and then I collapse against Riley's mailbox, panting for breath. I glance back at the house, steeling myself for what's about to burst through the front door.

But the house just sits there silently, its windows dark. Blood doesn't ooze beneath the front door; cockroaches don't swarm the porch. The perfectly trimmed bushes rustle in the stale air, then go still.

As I run from the house, the curtain at Riley's window flutters, like it's saying goodbye.

# CHAPTER TWENTY-SEVEN

I stumble through Riley's neighborhood, lost as to what to do next. Every towering house lining the street looks exactly like the one next to it, and I picture that each one is filled with the same horrors. I wrap my arms around my chest, trying not to shiver. I still have to find Riley. If that's what Brooklyn did to her house, I can't imagine what she has in mind for Riley herself.

Helplessness washes over me. I crouch on the street curb and lower my chin to my hands, trying to keep myself calm. I don't know Riley well enough to know where she'd go instead of home. To Josh's place, maybe? But no, Alexis said they broke up. My throat tightens as

I realize that all of Riley's other friends are dead.

I lean forward, and something in my pocket crunches. I cringe, thinking of the cockroaches. I reach into my pocket and pull out a crumpled piece of paper.

It's the photograph of Riley and her friends at the lake house. I consider it for a long moment. Alexis wears a white bikini, her smooth, perfect skin tanned to a deep golden brown. Riley sits next to her, her hair tied back with a silk scarf. They all look so perfect. Like people from a magazine.

Riley said she went to the lake house when she wanted to be alone. It's near Lake Whitney, half an hour away by car. Too far to walk. I need a ride.

I consider trying to take Mom's car, then dismiss the idea almost immediately. With the paramedics and Grace's body, our driveway is probably still a mob scene.

I slip my cell phone out of my sweatshirt pocket, quickly pulling up Charlie's number. I picture Charlie's bright red truck, and my thumb hovers nervously over the screen.

Finally, I work up the nerve to send him a text: *can u pick me up? its an emergency.*

I give him Riley's address and hit send. Then I wait. Less than a minute later, the phone vibrates in my hand.

*Be there in 10.*

I weave my hands together anxiously. Every passing

second feels like the difference between saving Riley's life and letting her die.

"Hurry," I whisper under my breath. I slip the phone into my pocket and walk to the porch. I tug my sweatshirt over my hands and crouch on the top step, drawing my knees up to my chest.

Luckily, it doesn't take ten minutes for Charlie's red truck to roll down the street and slow to a stop in front of Riley's house. Charlie throws the door open and jumps out without cutting the engine. He's wearing faded jeans and a sweatshirt, and his hair sticks up in all directions.

"Sofia? What is it? Are you okay?" He stops in front of me and reaches for my shoulder, but I immediately pull away. I feel dirty, like all the horrors of this weekend are streaked across my face. Like he'll know what I've done just by looking at me.

"I need to borrow your car."

"What?" Charlie frowns, and the dimple disappears from his cheek.

"It's a long story. But I need to go somewhere. Now."

He leans in and kisses me on the forehead. Just a couple of days ago this would have made my stomach flip, but now it feels like something I've stolen. I don't deserve a guy like Charlie.

"You can tell me the long story on the drive," he says. "I'll take you wherever you need to go."

I start to shake my head before he's even finished speaking. Hurt flashes across his face.

"Look," I say. "You can't come. I can't explain why right now, but you just . . . you can't."

Charlie's frown deepens. "Sofia, if you're in some kind of trouble, I want to help."

"You *can't*." This comes out sounding more frantic than I intend for it to, but I can't help it. I'm running out of time. "Charlie, you're a really nice guy, but you're better off without me."

Charlie laughs and reaches for me again. "That's not true."

I lean away from him, pressing against his truck. "It is true," I say, slipping my fingers into the door latch. "I've done terrible things. You'd hate me if you knew. You'll probably hate me for this, too, but it's for the best."

Charlie shakes his head. "What are you talking about?"

I don't answer. Instead, I open the car door behind my back and slip into the front seat, pulling the door closed. Before he can reach for the latch himself, I hit the lock.

"Sorry!" I yell. Charlie bangs against the glass, and the muffled *fwump fwump* echoes through the truck.

"Sofia!" he shouts, but his voice sounds far away. I shift the truck into drive. If I see how betrayed he looks,

I know I won't be able to do this. I close my eyes when I hit the gas and keep them closed when the truck lurches forward.

By the time I open them again, my vision is clouded with tears, and I wouldn't be able to see his face anyway.

* * *

I look up *Lake Whitney* on my cell while I drive, and follow the directions to a misty flat park surrounded by dense woods. I slow Charlie's truck as the road narrows and curves into the trees. The moon peeks over the distant hills and reflects off the steely lake, turning the trees gray and silver through the fog.

Houses line the waterfront, and just as I start to worry that I'll never find Riley in time, the road curves again, ending in front of a private beach and a thick cove of fir trees. Beyond the tops of the trees, I see a dark, slate-colored roof and chimney. I shift the truck into park and push the door open, but I leave the engine running, like Charlie did. Riley and I might have to make a quick getaway. Shoving my hands in my sweatshirt pockets, I hurry down the rocky gravel driveway.

I immediately recognize Riley's family's lake house from the photograph. It's a low, sprawling cabin made of weathered gray wood. Floor-to-ceiling windows cover one entire side of the house, showing a darkened room filled with sleek, modern furniture. A narrow wooden dock stretches far out into the lake. I picture Riley and Alexis spreading their beach towels across the wood and slow to a walk. I'm sure this is the right place. But it looks empty.

Then something moves on the porch, and I turn, narrowing my eyes.

Riley's huddled beneath a blanket on one of the wooden chairs, holding a cup of tea. She flinches when she sees me walking toward her, then sets the teacup on the ground and stands. The blanket drops from her shoulders.

"Sofia." Her voice cracks when she says my name. "Oh my god. I thought . . ."

She lets the end of her sentence trail off, but I know what she was going to say. She thought I'd died in that house with Brooklyn. She thought the fire had killed me.

"We have to go." I don't mean for my voice to sound flat and angry, but it does. As relieved as I am that Riley's not hurt, I can't just forget what happened last night—the fact that she left me to burn, the things she did to Brooklyn and to me.

She studies my face, and something inside her cracks. Tears pour down her cheeks.

"Sofia, things got really out of control," she says. "I don't know what . . ."

The truck's engine sputters, interrupting her. I step forward and grab her arm.

"We can talk about all that later," I tell her, glancing nervously over my shoulder. "But right now we have to get out of here."

Riley frowns. "Why? What's wrong?"

"Grace," I say. "She's dead."

Riley's eyes widen in horror. She takes a step back. "No."

"It was Brooklyn," I continue. "You were right about her all along. She's evil. She killed Grace, and now she's coming after you."

Riley lifts a hand to her mouth. The quiet unnerves me, and goose bumps rise on the back of my neck. I wrap my arms around my chest.

That's when I realize—the car engine. I don't hear it anymore.

"Oh, god," I whisper. I turn around and take a few steps back over the rocky driveway. Riley's feet crunch over the gravel behind me. When I see the spot in front of the beach where Charlie's truck is still parked, I freeze.

Brooklyn leans against the hood, tossing the car keys from hand to hand. When she sees me, she smiles.

"Hey, Sofia," she says. "Catch."

And she throws the keys into the lake.

# CHAPTER TWENTY-EIGHT

Brooklyn steps away from the truck. Her smile is all teeth, and the longer I stare at it, the more it looks like a grimace. Brooklyn ripped the skin off Riley's face with those teeth. My knees buckle, and I nearly fall to the ground right there.

"Oh, god." Riley releases her breathe in a hiss. "Brooklyn."

Brooklyn wrinkles her nose. Her feet crunch over the gravel. "Hey, lover. Miss me?"

"Brooklyn, think about this," I beg, but she steps past me like I'm not there. A hammer sticks out of the waistband of her jeans. My stomach turns. No one blocks my path to the dirt road now. I could run to the main street and flag down a car. It was what Riley did to me in that burning house. It would be poetic, almost. The muscles in my legs tense to run.

Flames crackle beneath Brooklyn's toes. With every step she takes, she leaves a curl of fire behind her. It burns blue at first, but then the fire crawls over the white gravel in the driveway and its edges burn orange and red.

Any hope I had of running vanishes with the growing flames. I had to know, on some level, that Brooklyn was capable of this. I saw what she did with the candle in the attic, but I let myself believe it was coincidence, luck. Now I stare at the fire, watching it curl into the air and lick the ground. It's evil—she's evil. There's nowhere I can run to escape her. No matter where I go, Brooklyn will find me.

"You like?" Brooklyn asks. Riley opens her mouth, then closes it again. Brooklyn frowns. "What's the matter? Aren't you impressed?"

"I—" Riley's body flies backward, and the words are ripped from her throat. She slams against the lake house wall. The gray siding shudders as she slides to the ground. She looks dead, but then she lifts a trembling hand to her face to push her hair out of her eyes.

Brooklyn stops a few yards away from the house.

Flames lick at her toes and feet, but she doesn't seem to feel them.

She lifts her arms, holding them out to her sides like a cross. In the dim light her skin looks ghostly white, and the injuries from Riley's knife and the matches stand out in stark contrast. The red cuts and clotted blood seem almost fake, like they were drawn on using that cheap, oily paint that comes with Halloween costumes.

Before my eyes, blood moves back into the wounds and disappears, and the skin stitches itself together, leaving behind only faded pink lines. The stub of her pinkie stretches and grows, becoming whole again. It's like watching one of those nature shows where time speeds up and a flower blooms in seconds. The evil hovers around us, thick and suffocating. I couldn't run now, not even if I wanted to. The air weighs down my limbs like mud, holding me in place.

Brooklyn's scars grow fainter, then disappear completely. She rubs her hands over her arms, grinning. "That was fun," she says.

Riley releases a choked sob. She lowers her head again, and her hair swings over her tear-stained face. She clenches her hands in front of her.

"Hail Mary," she whispers. "Mother of God . . ."

"Your God doesn't care what you have to say," Brooklyn snarls. "Now, do you want to see a real crucifixion?"

Brooklyn throws Riley's body backward, slamming it against the side of the house again. Riley's arms shoot out from her sides—forming a cross. She groans, struggling against some invisible barrier holding her in place. She releases a choked, terrified scream.

Brooklyn stands directly in front of Riley. Fire eats the earth behind her, crackling and spitting in the wind. Smoke turns the air hazy. It looks like a mirage.

Brooklyn glances at me and winks, like we're sharing a joke. She tugs the hammer out of the back of her jeans.

"Sofia, help me!" Riley screams. She throws her head against the wall behind her, making the wood crack. "Help me, help me, please!"

I want to look away, but I don't. It feels cowardly, like if I can't save Riley, the least I can do is watch her die. Maybe that's Brooklyn's joke. Once again I'm forced to watch something terrible happen, helpless to do anything to stop it.

Brooklyn's lips curl into a wicked smile. She pulls a long silver nail out of her pocket.

"Hold still." She positions the nail directly in front of Riley's palm. "This is going to hurt. A lot."

She swings the hammer, driving the nail deep into Riley's hand and pinning it to the house behind her. Riley screams. Brooklyn swings again and again. I imagine the nail piercing skin and bone and muscle. Bile rises in my throat. I scream, too. The sound rips from my body and echoes until my chest burns and my throat goes raw and my head aches.

I don't scream for Riley. I scream because I'm next.

"Now, *this* is a crucifixion," Brooklyn says. I wrench my head up in time to see Brooklyn position a nail over Riley's other hand and swing her hammer. I throw my hands over my face, clenching my eyes shut. I don't want to watch anymore, but my eyes flicker open and I stare at Riley and Brooklyn through the spaces in my fingers.

Riley's body slumps and her weight pulls against the nails in her hands. The fire has reached the house now. It spreads over the grass below and climbs the walls. Gray paint bubbles up beneath the flames.

"H . . . hail Mary . . ." I try to pray. But the words get stuck in my throat. I squeeze my eyes shut, trying to picture the statuette of the Virgin on my grandmother's windowsill. But I can't hold her in my head. It's like she's deserted me.

Brooklyn flips the hammer in her hand and digs the clawed edge deep into Riley's chest. Riley opens her mouth, but instead of speaking, she releases a wet, gurgling sound. Blood bubbles around her teeth. Brooklyn yanks the hammer through her ribs, ripping her thin white T-shirt to shreds. She relaxes her grip on the hammer, and it clatters to the driveway. Her arm shoots forward and she pulls something from Riley's chest.

A heart. Riley's heart.

Riley's head slumps forward. Still holding her heart, Brooklyn turns to face me.

My legs tense, but I don't run. There's not a place on earth I could run where Brooklyn wouldn't find me. I know what's going to happen next. If I stand here and face it, then at least I won't die a coward.

Brooklyn steps toward me. I try to be brave, but the sound of nails crunching through Riley's skin echoes in my head. When I close my eyes I see Grace strung up on the shed, her blood dripping onto the driveway. Brooklyn's not a fan of quick, easy deaths.

"Why so glum?" Brooklyn says. She drops Riley's heart, and it hits the ground with a heavy, wet thud. I stare at Brooklyn's shoulder, at the feathered tail of her Quetzalcoatl tattoo as she walks toward me. I focus on the tattoo to keep from picturing blood blossoming on Riley's T-shirt, or the half-circle gash on Grace's neck, or the way Alexis's fingers curled toward her palm. Still, my hands tremble. I don't want to die.

"Haven't you figured it out yet?" Brooklyn asks. She tucks a spiky strand of hair behind her ear. Blood coats her hand like a glove, and she leaves a line of red along her cheek.

"Figured what out?" I whisper. All around us the cicadas buzz.

Brooklyn pulls me close to her. She whispers into my ear, "The evil lives inside you already."

The buzzing insects become a train's whistle. I squeeze my eyes shut, trying to push the memory away. But I can't help it. Images of that night on the tracks flicker behind my closed eyes. I see the headlight in the distance. I hear Karen screaming.

*"Sofia, get off the tracks!" Karen drops her beer and grabs my arm, trying to pull me away. I don't move. The train honks again. I blink into the headlight. It's close enough now that I can't look at it directly.*

*"Oh my god!" Karen says. "Sofia, come on. This isn't funny!"*

*She tries to pull again, but this time I wrap my fingers around her wrist and tug her forward. She's so surprised that she stumbles onto the tracks next to me.*

*"Does it look like I'm fucking laughing?" I hiss at her, and I dive out of the way as the train crashes forward.*

I open my eyes, and Brooklyn's watching me, grinning. Something stirs inside me, something thick and suffocating. *No.* I scratch at my skin, leaving red marks along my wrists. The evil is inside me. I feel it. I scratch harder to tear it out of my body, drawing blood. In my head,

I hear my grandmother's raspy voice. *Diablo, Diablo* . . .

But then the feeling stretches, spreading up my spine and into my arms and legs. It uncurls in my chest like an animal. It feels warm now, powerful. Like fire. Brooklyn grabs my wrist. I stare at the trail of blood around my arm and feel something new. Hunger.

"You're not going to kill me," I say. It's not a question. I already know the answer.

"Don't be silly, Sofia," Brooklyn says, dropping my hand. Her eyes glow red, like she's lit from within. "We don't kill our own."

# ACKNOWLEDGMENTS

First of all, I'd like to thank one of my very favorite people, Rebecca Marsh, for having cool editor-like friends who don't seem to mind when you corner them at a birthday party and spend the entire night talking about how you really, really want to work with them. And, of course, an even bigger thanks to Emilia Rhodes, who didn't hold that against me, and who seemed to think that spending 45 minutes fan-girling over *Buffy the Vampire Slayer* qualified me to write a horror novel. To all of you wannabe writers out there who might be reading this, I really don't recommend this approach.

Next, I absolutely could not have written this book

without several hundred amazing people, most notably Josh Bank, Sara Shandler, and Katie Schwartz at Alloy, for being so supportive during the whole process, as well as Ben Schrank and Caroline Donofrio at Razorbill for some truly fantastic editorial notes and direction (also for the cookies. I feel like there have been a lot of cookies). Felicia Frazier, and the rest of Razorbill's sales, marketing and publicity team have also been amazingly supportive in ways I could not believe. After nearly five years working in children's book marketing, I know how many people it takes to make a book a book. Thank you all for helping me make mine!

I also have to thank my mother, who thought it was completely appropriate to let me watch Stephen King movies and read horror novels when I was still in grade school. Let's just chalk that up to research, okay? Thanks, also, to the rest of my fantastic friends and family, for letting me complain when things were hard and building me up when I got low. Seriously, I know the best people ever.

And, finally, I have to thank my husband, Ronald, for reading every pass, even though he hates horror. Prepare yourself, babe. The next one's going to be even scarier.

WE'RE ALL GONNA DIE DOWN HERE

TURN THE PAGE FOR A SNEAK PEEK. . . .

# ONE

**DEAD PEOPLE DON'T REALLY LOOK LIKE THEY'RE** sleeping.

I'm not an expert. I've only seen the one. She was my roommate at Mountainside Gardens Rehabilitation Center. Rachel, only she pronounced her name *Rock-el*. I used to say it wrong on purpose.

Rachel was a boozehound. I had to dump all my perfume because the nurses said she'd drink it once withdrawal set in. I thought they were full of it, but then Rachel found out this girl down the hall had nail polish remover. She snuck out one night and stole it.

I found her in our bathroom, slumped next to the toilet. Sweat drenched her bleached-blond hair, making it clump around her hollowed-out cheeks and blue-tinted face. Skinny red veins spiderwebbed over the whites of her eyes, and blood and snot dripped from her nose. Dried vomit clung to her chin and her cracked purple lips.

I didn't tell anyone outside of the clinic about Rachel. Not my parents. Not even Shana.

I also didn't tell anyone back home about Moira, who ate her own hair, or Cara, who screamed whenever you touched her, or Tori Anne, who begged for drugs even though all her teeth were rotting out of her skull. You can't tell people stories like that without giving them ideas.

Like, *That's really fucked up.*

Or, *What were you even doing there?*

Or, *Maybe you're just like them.*

"End of the road," I say. "Last house on the left."

Dad pulls our Subaru around the corner, past a wooden sign that reads FLYING EAGLE ESTATES. I press my face against the car window. Identical brick mini mansions spiral off in every direction, all surrounded by lush green grass and towering pine trees. When I was little, I used to think Madison's neighborhood looked like something out of a fairy tale. We'd spend hours darting across the pristine lawns and hiding behind gnarled old oak trees, pretending to be warrior princesses.

"I remember where Madison lives, Casey," Dad says. "You used to spend every weekend here."

I twirl the turtle charm on my necklace. I got it because of my last name, Myrtle, and also because I was going to

study them back when I was planning on being a
biologist. But marine biology means college, so who
knows anymore. "You excited to see your friends?" Dad
asks.

"Sure." I stretch the word into two syllables. How
excited can you be to see "parent-approved" friends? I
mean, really? Dad shoots me a look. "I *am*," I add, flashing my "normal teenage girl" smile. "Really."

Dad nods, but he doesn't look convinced. We have the
same face: long, straight nose, stubby chin. We even have
the same dark eyes and thick brows that tell the world
exactly what we're thinking at every moment. Right now,
his brows pinch in at the middle, creating tiny worry lines
on his forehead.

I flip down the sun visor and scrutinize my reflection.
Pale skin, circles under my eyes, and a fresh zit coming
in on my forehead. I should have insisted on a post-rehab
makeover.

I push my hair back to check out the freshly shaved
side of my head. At least that still looks badass. I stole my
dad's electric razor a couple of days after getting back and
buzzed my brown locks. You can't see it when my hair is
down, but Mom freaked anyway. Which was the entire
point.

I make a face at my reflection and pinch my pale
cheeks. A faint burst of red appears on my skin, then
disappears a second later. I sigh and flip the sun visor up.

"Feeling okay?" Dad asks.

Translation: *Did the thousands of dollars we spent on Mountainside actually fix you?*

"I'm good. This is pie." Pie's my word. Kind of like "it's a piece of cake," only I used to scarf down these cherry–cream cheese pies my dad made every weekend.

It's also my classic nonanswer, and I feel guilty the second it's out of my mouth. "I feel stronger," I add.

"Well, I guess I'm glad," Dad says. I reach for the air conditioner and Dad drops his hand on mine before I can pull it away. He squeezes, his eyes still on the road. I let him leave his hand there for a full three seconds before shrugging it off.

We roll up to a white house with forest-green shutters and a wraparound front porch. Madison leans against one of the columns flanking the front door, her long, tan legs stretched out before her. All my old friends and soccer teammates crowd around her, talking and laughing.

It feels stuffy in the Subaru all of a sudden. I switch the air-conditioning off and roll my window down. Dad cuts the steering wheel to the left, pulling up alongside a row of freshly planted yellow tulips. I squirm, uncomfortably, in my seat.

"Something wrong?" Dad asks.

"No," I say, too fast. It's a scientific fact that dads don't understand teenage girl politics. Like how your former best friend might invite you to a sleepover just to be nice, and not because she actually wants to spend the night with the school cautionary tale.

I grab my polka-dot Herschel backpack and push the door open. The smell of tulips overwhelms me. It's like the way you imagine flowers smell, not how they *really* smell. Except these do.

Madison turns at the sound of the car door slamming. I step onto her lawn, and her face lights up.

"Casey!" she squeals. "You came!"

She hands her lemonade glass to the girl standing next to her and races across the sloped lawn toward me. Watching her, I feel a phantom twinge of pain in my knee, the injury that started this all. Madison throws her arms around my shoulders, and suddenly all I can see is tan skin and blond hair. She squeezes too tightly, giving me the feeling this hug is more for the girls on the porch and my dad than it is for me. I rock back on my heels.

"*Oof,*" I groan. She's not much larger than me, but she works out six times a week and never eats junk food. Her body is all muscle. *Life* is a contact sport for Madison.

Dad unrolls the car window. "Madison, it's nice to see you again," he says. Madison releases me from her strangle-hug. She's already wearing a pair of polka-dot pajama shorts and a loose-fitting T-shirt. He turns back to me and his eyebrows do the furrowing, worry-line thing again. "You have your cell, right? You'll call me if you need . . ."

"Anything," I finish for him. "I know. I will."

Dad stares at me for a beat too long, a nervous smile on his face. I should feel guilty about that smile. But I'm so tired of everyone looking at me like I'm a bomb about to go off.

I already *went* off. I'm better now.

Dad rolls his window up, waving one last time as he steers the car away from the curb. I wiggle my fingers at his taillights, halfheartedly.

"There's lemonade on the porch," Madison says, looping her arm around my shoulder. "And hummus and stuff."

She winds her thick blond braid around her finger. The gold "best friends" bracelet I gave her back in sixth grade dangles from her wrist. Something about it makes me sad. Like the strangle-hug made me sad. She's trying too hard to remind me that we're friends.

"Do you have Funfetti icing?" I ask, looking away from the bracelet. Funfetti was practically a fifth food group our freshman year.

"Ha," Madison says, and flicks the pendant on her bracelet. "Is it weird being back?"

"No, it's pie." I smooth my hair over the shaved side of my head. Shana said my old haircut didn't match my personality, but Madison wouldn't understand. She hasn't changed her hair since elementary school. "I'm doing good. Great, actually." I stop walking and lower my voice so the girls on the porch don't overhear me. "Look, I'm not really a drug addict. My parents overacted. They thought I was, like, shooting heroin into my eyeballs or something." I laugh, but it's stilted and awkward. Madison stares at me, frowning.

"Anyway," I continue, clearing my throat. "I just had a bad reaction to my painkillers." At least, I *think* I had a bad reaction to my painkillers. The night I went to rehab is a blank spot on my memory. I don't remember anything that happened, but Shana told me I passed out, and she said it could have been the pain meds, which is good enough for me. Apparently it happens all the time.

"I wasn't anything like the girls there," I finish, thinking of Rachel and Moira and Tori Anne.

Madison wrinkles her nose. She looks skeptical. "Painkillers can be addictive."

"Hence the rehab," I say. "And they were prescription, anyway." My doctor prescribed oxycodone after a girl the size of a Clydesdale slammed into me during a soccer game last year, ruining my knee. "My parents just flipped because I passed out, but my doctor said lots of people have bad reactions. It wasn't a big deal."

"I don't know. I'm not even eating white flour anymore," Madison says. "I read this article that says it's basically as addictive as cocaine."

I tug on my Myrtle necklace. What are you supposed to say to a girl who doesn't eat *bread*? That's not even human.

"Is there rehab for pasta?" I ask. Madison laughs too loudly for my stupid joke and takes the steps to the porch two at a time.

All the girls are already dressed in their pajamas, except for Stacy Donovan, who's wearing Nike athletic shorts and a neon blue sports bra. I'm pretty sure she was born wearing athletic shorts and a sports bra. She smiles at me when I step onto the porch.

"Cute jeans!" she calls.

"Um, thanks," I say. A pair of tight, dark-wash jeans with a ripped knee hangs low on my hips, accentuating my long legs and thin waist. I spent all afternoon trying on everything in my closet, and I finally landed on my best jeans and a slouchy black T-shirt.

"Do you want to get changed?" Madison asks. I glance down at my backpack. I brought my matching pj's with the giant strawberries on them, like I'm twelve.

"I'm good for now." I dump my backpack on the ground and take the glass of lemonade Madison offers me.

Kiki Charles waves from the porch swing, where she's sitting with Amanda Rice and a girl from the JV team I don't recognize. I wave back. Kiki and I used to partner up for early morning sprints, and Amanda always offered to paint my nails blue and yellow—the team colors—on the bus to away games. But that was all pre-injury, pre-Shana, pre-rehab. I barely saw them after I quit the team last year.

Amanda leans forward, balancing her lemonade glass on her knee. "Please tell me you're taking calc this year," she says. "Algebra 2 was horrible after you left. Mr. Nelson was up to two puns a day by the end of the year, and I had no one to groan with in the back row."

"Tragic," I say, and the corner of my mouth lifts into a smile. Talking about school is the high school girl equivalent of talking about the weather. But it's still better than the alternative.

"You have no idea," Amanda says. "Did you know he likes angles, but only to a certain *degree*? Ooh, and he kept threatening to kick Kevin Thomas out of class if he had another infraction." She shoots me a disgusted look over the top of her lemonade glass. "Get it? In*fraction*."

Madison rolls her eyes. "No one has suffered like you've suffered," she says.

I take a drink of lemonade, grimacing as I swallow. It's sugar-free. "So." I clear my throat, shrugging the tension from my shoulders. "What else have I missed?"

"Tuesday's now sloppy joe day in the cafeteria," Madison says with mock enthusiasm. "And Sean Davenport's dating Clare Ryan this week, so that's . . . special."

I frown, trying to picture our high school quarterback with Clare, the drama weirdo who wears a beret to school every day. "What happened to Sarah?"

"Sarah's a born-again Christian now," Kiki explains, wrinkling her nose. "That's a whole different drama. Oh, and Sam cut his hair. Have you seen—"

"I'm so behind already," I say, interrupting her before she can start talking about my ex-boyfriend. Madison slips an arm over my shoulder.

"I went to junior prom with Henry Frank and he spent the *entire* night making out with Lisa Jones in the third-floor stairwell," she says.

"Asshole." I tuck my hair behind my ear, flashing her a smile. I know she's trying to steer the conversation away from Sam, and I feel a rush of gratitude. It's almost like old times. Like in fifth grade when this girl in the cafeteria made fun of me for getting ketchup on my white tank top, and Madison retaliated by dumping a carton of chocolate milk over her head.

Then Amanda Rice leans forward, wrinkling her nose. "Did you shave your head?" she asks.

*Shit*. I push my fingers through my hair and touch the buzzed sides of my head. It feels like peach fuzz. "Not exactly."

"Did you do it in rehab?" Amanda asks. Madison shoots her a look—her "we talked about this" look. Which means they must've had an entire conversation about me before I even got here.

I look down at the ice melting in my lemonade glass, trying to ignore the heat climbing up the back of my neck.

I imagine Madison telling them not to ask me about rehab. Madison saying they should pretend everything's normal. That we're all still friends.

"It was just a question," Amanda mutters.

I smooth my hair over my ears. "I didn't do it in rehab."

"It looks, um, really different," Madison says in a fake cheery voice. "But whatever, right? It's just hair. It'll grow back."

"Yeah." I fumble with Myrtle and look down at my shoes. You should be allowed to scream in public whenever a conversation gets really awkward. And then time could reset itself and you get a do-over.

But I can't scream without everyone thinking I'm a crazy junkie, so I pinch the skin on my palm and stare at the mole in the middle of Amanda's forehead. She's still talking but her voice sounds like static. All I hear is a low buzz as she drones on.

The sound of a motor cuts through the hum. I turn to watch a rusty sky-blue Buick rumble up the street. I grin, recognizing Shana's car immediately. She inherited it when her grandmother got too old to drive. Her grandmother's CHASTITY IS FOR LOVERS sticker still decorates the back bumper, but Shana scratched out "lovers" with her keys and carved "fuckers" into the paint next to it. She left her grandmother's rosaries dangling from the rearview mirror but hot-glued the head of her little sister's My Little Pony to the car antenna.

Shana pulls up next to the curb, and the little horsey head wobbles above the car like crazy. Obnoxiously loud rock music drifts out of her cracked windows. Julie fills her cheeks with air and presses her lips against the back window. Aya sits next to her, eyes squeezed shut as she croons along with the music.

"Oy, Case!" Shana hollers. She honks, twice. "Get that cute little ass down here!"

The soccer girls go silent. Madison frowns.

"Are they drunk?" she asks.

"No," I say, although they probably are. Julie fogs up the back window with her breath and draws a penis in the steam. She doubles over with laughter. I start to smile, too, then bite my lip when I see the look on Madison's face.

"What are they *doing* here?"

"I don't know," I say. I really don't. I haven't seen Shana since getting back from rehab. She must've called my house to figure out where I was.

"Casey!" Shana lays on her horn. Without realizing I'm doing it, I pull my backpack up over my shoulder.

Madison freezes, a carrotful of hummus halfway to her mouth. "Wait, are you *leaving* with them?"

"I . . ." I hesitate.

The thing is, I never worry that Shana talks about me behind my back. If she had something to say, she'd say it to my face. And Shana would never invite me out just to be nice. Shana repels "nice" like water repels oil. She's the antithesis of nice. She's *real*.

I glance back at her car. She stares at me from the front seat, one eyebrow cocked. Like a dare.

"I'm sorry," I finish lamely.

"Whatever." Madison picks up her lemonade, shaking the ice at the bottom of the glass. The best friend charm glints on her wrist.

"The next time you have a sleepover . . ." I start, but Madison snorts and gives me a look that's pure venom.

"Sorry," I say again. I set my lemonade glass on the porch railing and start down the steps.

"Casey," Madison calls. I stop at the edge of her lawn and glance over my shoulder.

"Yeah?"

Madison stares at Shana's Buick. For a split second, I see things like she does: the rusted car that could break down at any moment, Shana drumming her hands against the steering wheel. Julie lighting a joint in the backseat.

Madison shifts her eyes back to me. I wind the backpack strap around my fingers, suddenly uncomfortable. I think of Rachel's puffy face and bloodshot eyes and have to clench my shoulders to keep from visibly cringing. I can't imagine what Madison sees when she looks at me. Only that I don't belong on her perfect lawn or in her perfect life. Not anymore.

Madison just shakes her head. "Be safe," she mutters.